Panther in the Sun

PANTHER IN THE SUN

John Comfort

bg

BOOK GENESIS PRESS

Prologue

It was a sunny spring day and the wind nipped at young Panther in the Sun's fresh face, reminding him of the winter that had just passed. Panther walked proudly, side-by-side with his father. He listened to his father's words intently with his thirteen-year old ears as they made their way towards the edge of their mandated land—a Sioux Reservation in South Dakota. The year was 1913, and life was becoming harder and harder for Panther and his family on the plains. Today's walk was like most, except his father had a deeper curiosity and concern that fueled him to walk to the outermost land of their reservation. His father had continually heard of the white men breaking treaty and settling on reservation land given to the Sioux.

"Crouch down and look, my son," Whispers of the Wind said quietly with serious eyes. They both crouched down in the now tall green grass and peered out over a settlement. It was a sparse, white man's homesteading village that was further pushing onto their reservation.`

"Why do they keep coming?" Panther in the Sun asked with puzzled paranoia in his voice.

"Because they don't respect us. And they will keep coming. And they will keep pushing," his father told his son in a very calm, matter-of-fact way. "Come. Stay low. I want to get close enough to see faces."

Panther nodded and followed his father. He adjusted his knife by his side to match the perfect positioning of his father's knife. They moved slowly and invisibly. As they approached the end of the grass line, Panther's father motioned for him to stop. They both peeked out and took in the activity of the village. It was just another day for the homesteaders. The men went about constructing small houses as the women could be seen cleaning and minding the activity of the children. Panther momentarily smiled as he watched a little kid fall while playing with his friends. His father looked over with a different face. A face Panther understood. A face of despair.

"Let's go," his father said. "I've seen enough. No need to . . ."

"No need to what?" a white man said with a smirk as he popped up from tall grass behind a large tree. He pointed a pistol with one hand and held onto his flask with another. Both Panther and his father froze and calmly lifted their hands into the air as the man rose up. "Out for a little walk, huh? Bad luck for you, stumblin' upon a man drinkin' whisky with a gun. Kind of unfortunate I had to be here, upwind and all, huh?" the man said as he slowly approached Whispers of the Wind with the gun pointed at his head.

"Yes," Whispers of the Wind calmly said as he guided Panther behind his back.

"Oh, that's Junior. Taking him on his first scalping? In the middle of the day?" he inquired sarcastically with increasing anger in his voice and stepped to within a couple of feet of his father.

"No. Just a walk on our land. The very same land you are attempting to illegally settle on."

"Well, sorry to be the bearer of bad news, but this will be the last

2

time you walk. Injun land, or not. You too, Junior. Sorry, nothing personal against your people. In fact, I prefer Injun girls, especially dem young ones," he said with an evil grin and a tilt of his head. He cocked his pistol. Panther's heart raced and a burst of energy he had never felt overtook him. He quickly jumped out and rolled with a yell. The man instantly moved the gun towards him, but was cut short by Whispers of the Wind. He swiftly took control of the man's hand and arm. A shot was fired wildly and whizzed by Panther's head. Young Panther, now frozen in fear, watched as his father fought for both of their lives. Devastating blows were exchanged and Panther couldn't move. "Move! Move!" Panther screamed at himself on the inside. He stared at the fallen gun. Then stared back at the commotion. "Panther!" his father yelled. Panther snapped out of it and saw his father on top of the man in an attempt to plunge his knife into the white man's chest, but was being held back with great strength. Panther quickly picked up the revolver and moved over and pointed it at the man's head.

"Do it!" the man screamed as spit and snot bubbles spilled out. "Do it!" Panther quickly looked at his father and his father quickly back at him.

"No!" his father mustered from the depths of his soul. And with that, his father plunged his knife deep into the man's shoulder, sparing the man's life. He delivered a fierce blow to the man's head, knocking him unconscious. Panther instantly went back into a state of shock as the gun fell from his shaking hands. His father removed the knife and wiped the blood onto the man's clothes. He stood up, out of breath, covered in mud and the man's blood. He looked at Panther, sheathed his knife, and walked the few steps to his son. He coaxed his son out of shock with a hug and then words of urgency.

"We must run. A shot was fired. I'm proud of you, son. Let's go." Panther instantly reacted to his father's words and they ran back to the safety of their village.

1

WHEN PANTHER IN THE SUN WAS NINETEEN YEARS OLD, HE LOST BOTH his mother and father to smallpox in the same year. Panther still replayed his first violent encounter with the white man. He would never forget it. Nor would he ever forget his father. His despair and longing to be by his side again could only be shared with his grandfather—his only living family. Panther's angst grew with each passing day. Everywhere he turned, he saw the destruction of his people.

"I can't stay here anymore, grandfather, you see what's happening to our people. They've forced us into this box, stolen everything that we've held sacred, and now they want our souls," Panther in the Sun said, as he sat with his grandfather inside their teepee on the Lakota Sioux Reservation. Panther had become a strikingly handsome young Native American man. He sat with his legs crossed, back upright, hair pulled back into a single long braid and kept intense eye contact with his grandfather, Eagle's Claw.

"They can't take our souls, but, yes, they will try," Eagle's Claw said, as he packed his pipe with fresh tobacco.

"They have driven our people to alcohol, killed our people, including my mother and father, with their disease and our children are now listening to their teachings," Panther said as he clinched his fists. "They even want us to fight their wars."

"Yes, this is true. I have held on for so long, and will continue to do so, even in this box. It's the only way I know. It is up to our people to not let our ways die. They can take our land, and impose their laws, but they will not take our souls," he said with great strength behind his seventy-year old eyes.

"Yes, but what do we do? When all of our resources are dependent upon the white man, and our men are becoming weak with their ways? We are losing. Look around us, we have already lost," he said and stood up angry.

"Have you lost? Have you lost what your father and I have given you?" Eagle's Claw asked his grandson.

"No, I haven't, and I never will either," he said with great strength behind his now-twenty-year old eyes, only a young man.

"So, what is it that you are going to do for our people? You are the generation to make a change. If the change is not here, then maybe it will be somewhere else. That will be your choice."

"Well, I know this, grandfather, I can't stay here in this box. I will not be told where to live, and that's what I will do for our people. I will not be confined, and I will hold my ways until the day that I die. I'm going to beat them at their own game, and go on the offensive, because I've been sitting down too long."

"Be careful in your words, grandson, offense isn't always the best defense. Be cautious, do not get wrapped into their ways, which can happen if you play their game. Are you to go?"

"Yes, grandfather, I am. I will make our people proud in all that I do. I will make my father proud, and my grandfather proud," he said as he knelt down to him in respect. "If only my father were here, he would see my strength."

"He already does. He watches as we speak," Eagle's Claw said and held his grandson's head against his own. "Return to me in short time, and tell me what you find."

"Yes, grandfather, I will," Panther said as he rose and left the teepee. He walked straight out of the reservation, only with the clothes on his back, and a small bag strapped around his shoulders alongside his bow. He was determined to live a free life, one free of the indoctrination, institutionalization, and confinement of the reservation. He carried on his shoulders not only his pack, but the pride of his people, and the self-imposed as well as generational expectation of his father and grandfather to carry on the way of the Sioux, no matter what. His heart was heavy with the troubles of his people, but his mind was strong and confident that he alone could make a difference in one way or another, a difference that would only transpire outside the walls of the reservation. Panther in the Sun didn't know which way to turn, as he continued his walk out. He had little in his possession—a hatchet, a bow with a quiver of arrows, a blanket, and no money. His feet were strapped with moccasins, and his body covered with the deerskin clothes his mother had made him before she died. He held his parents close to his heart with the necklace he wore. He didn't know what direction to travel, nor did he know what he was looking for and wouldn't know until he grasped the guidance from the Great Spirit. So, in the meantime, he headed west to a land he had never seen. He wanted to know, he wanted to find, and he wanted to be free.

Since he was a child, Panther in the Sun had been taught the ways of his people. He was taught humility, bravery, kindness, and love. He was taught respect for the earth, and how to live in harmony with it, so that it would keep giving. He learned to listen to the wind, feel the grass beneath his feet, and taste the goodness that mother earth provided for him and all mankind. He learned that no man was greater than the next, and that all were born equal. He learned pride for his people, and that there was nothing you wouldn't do to protect those that you loved. He learned that war was necessary, and that the Sioux Nation was once a great warrior nation. To be a warrior brought great honor to your people, and that when confronted with opposition that refused a peaceful resolution, then war was an absolute necessity. Panther in the Sun had never seen war, nor many of the things his ancestors saw. But he did see the destruction that the white man brought upon his people, and the war they waged was not out of necessity, or because the opposition could not reach a peaceful resolution, but it was out of greed and lack of respect for earth and mankind that they waged their war. He learned above all things to believe in himself, and this is what he set out to do, believe in himself, and rely upon himself while representing his great nation. These are the things that he knew, this is who he was, and this empowered him. He did, however, want to know more, and he wanted to find out what his own personal truth was.

He traveled west into Montana, taking game as he went along to survive, sleeping under the big sky full of stars. He wanted freedom, and freedom he had. There was no one in sight for hundreds of miles, no one to tell him what to do, where to go, or how to do anything. The land was open, not like the day of his people, but the freedom was felt in his mind. His heart was wounded from the intrusion of the white man, and he knew nothing else, as he was born into a white world. He sat one night by his fire and listened to the silence. A silence he had never really heard before, and though peaceful, it was frightening. He had always had someone to talk to, now it was just him and the stars. He laid back onto the grass that summer night of 1920, and talked to the only one listening—himself.

"Where is my place?" he asked out loud. "What am I to do? When all is conquered and owned, where is my place? I cannot be contained, and won't be, so stop trying," he pled his case to the sky, hoping that someone was listening. He had always been taught that someone would listen—his ancestors or the Great Spirit, but that night he felt alone. He started to think about the origin of man's aggression in a way he had never thought about it before. He was trying to figure out how and why everyone fought over land. He remembered the stories of his ancestors coming down from Alaska, migrating to new land. He thought about all the stories of wars with other tribes, and began to wonder how it was so different from what the white man had done. He quickly dismissed the idea, because the white man actually claimed the land as their own, when his people felt that no one could own the earth; it was everyone's to share. But tribes made claim to territory, and would go to war for it just the same. His people didn't buy and sell land, but they surely fought for it. He started to wonder about mankind in general, and was it just the white people? And were all white people ruthless, heartless savages? Surely other types of people warred with others, including their own type of people. It must be a survival of the fittest, or survival of the ones with the biggest weapons. As long as there is man, there will be war. The hatred for the white man was related to their lack of mercy, their abuse of the earth, and their mass destruction without remorse. He knew of tribes that behaved similarly, and began to wonder if it wasn't necessarily about color, but about the types of people. Just like his people showed kindness, mercy, and respect, maybe there were other people who did the same. He remembered the story of Rain in the Face, and the day a white man released him from his chains. Maybe there were others like him.

"How do I become stronger? How is it that I'm going to fit in, without giving in? We were defeated, but I'm not going to be. I respect my ancestors, but I am here now, undefeated," he said as he stood up and saw a shooting star darting through the sky, racing to the east. He took it as a sign, a sign to be free and use it as his guide. He was a human, a human in a race, and he wasn't going to lose. He was determined to find goodness in mankind, no matter the color, and not wallow in the past. He was born into this world just like anyone else. This was his life, and he wasn't going to live it in any type of box.

He woke in the morning, and headed in the direction of the falling star. He traveled for days and days, staying hidden in the woods as he traveled, until he reached the land of the Illinois. He camped by a small lake surrounded by woods, wondering what he was to do next, and then his answer was given. He looked into the sun, and there she was. A woman of such beauty, that she outshined the rays that pierced the clouds. His heart skipped a beat as she moved nearer.

"Hello," she said, and Panther in the Sun jumped to his feet.

"Hello," he said to her in English.

"Are you lost?" the young woman asked and then looked back towards the open field of grass, making sure of something.

"No, I'm not. I followed a star that fell from the sky, and it guided me here," he said and looked out onto the water.

"I'm Anna, what's your name?" she asked, as she looked at him with her gorgeous green eyes.

"I'm Panther in the Sun," he said and stood tall.

"O.k., well, nice to meet you. Where are you from, and where are you going?"

"I'm from the land of my people, and I'm going to wherever the Great Spirit leads me, and for now, that's here."

"Oh, o.k., well how about a hot meal? I'll check with my mom and dad, and then come back. o.k.?"

"No, no, that's o.k., thank you anyways," he said not knowing what type of situation or people he would encounter.

"It's o.k., really, we're good people. Let me ask. Here, come on," she said with an intoxicating smile. Panther in the Sun thought about it for a moment, and then followed her. They walked as the sun began to set, and the wildflowers swayed in the breeze. They neared the home, and then were at the door. His heart started to pound, as she stood at the farm house door. She opened it, and he froze where he stood.

"Come on, it's o.k.," she said with the same enticing smile, and he followed. The door opened to a home mixed with the familiar and foreign, and then the people he saw were gentle. "Mom, this is Panther in the Sun," Anna said as she introduced him while her mother cooked in the kitchen.

"Hello," the pretty white woman said kindly and then continued to cook.

"He followed a star that lead him here," she said and then smiled at Panther. It was at this point that her mother put down her spoon and took time to further acknowledge the young man standing in her home.

"Oh, is that right? Sit down, and tell me all about it," she said with a smile for the stranger.

"Anna, you fetch your father and brother; it's time for supper," she said and Panther's heart started to beat even harder. "It's o.k., young man, you're in good company," she said kindly. "Can I take your sack?"

"Um, yes, thank you," he said as she stood to take off his load and place it near him. He settled his bow by his feet, along with his arrows, and tried to be present. After just a few short moments, both Anna's father and brother came in.

"Hello," the tall, strong, Native American man said and extended his hand to a rising Panther in the Sun. They shook hands as they locked eyes, seeing a bit of their own selves in each other. Panther then looked to Anna, seeing the same thing.

"Hello," Panther said.

"Hi, I'm Jack," Anna's brother said and extended his hand as well, seeing the same in his brownish-green eyes.

"Hello," Panther said and shook his hand.

"So, let's eat, huh?" Anna's father said with a smile. They ate and carried on, like long lost friends, and Panther in the Sun felt very at home.

"So, Panther, what tribe are you from?" Anna's mom asked.

"I am Lakota Sioux," he said and then looked over to her husband.

"Oh, is that right, my husband is Dakota Sioux," she said and looked to her husband.

"Yes, I sure am," he said with a smile. "So, what brings you out this way?"

"I am on a journey to find myself in this new world," he said and looked around the table.

"Yes, aren't we all," Anna's father answered. "You know, I was about your age when I left our reservation, that was about twenty years ago. My father and grandfather both fought in the war against the white man, when I was just a boy."

"Why did you leave?" Panther ask respectfully.

"Well, much of the same reason as you, I guess. I had no one; my entire family was killed. So, I stayed with another family for a while, then I left first chance I got. I got a job at a factory and that's when I met Anna's grandfather, my wife's father. He was a very kind man, which I didn't think existed, and well, he allowed me to take out his daughter, and here we are today."

"Oh, I see," he said and continued to eat. "Thank you so much for the food."

"You're welcome, darlin'," Anna's mom said, and Anna smiled at the young man sitting at her family's table.

"My grandfather was a great warrior, right dad?" Jack, fifteen, asked as he looked to his father.

"Yes, he was, he was a very brave man."

"And so was your dad, right mom?"

"Yes, he was. And he was a very good man too, which can be one in the same," she said and smiled at Panther in the Sun.

"Well, thank you so much for your kindness, and hospitality, I should get going," Panther said as he rose from his chair.

"No, no wait, you should stay for some pie. Right, mom?" Anna said quickly and then looked to both her mother and then to Panther in the Sun.

"Yes, absolutely," she said as she looked at her daughter and Panther.

"Oh, well, o.k., thank you," he said and sat back down.

"Where are you going next?" Jack asked.

"I don't know, I'm just trying to find a place, a place where I belong."

"Have you considered becoming a citizen, Panther in the Sun?" the father asked.

"I already am, to the Sioux Nation," he answered.

"Yes, right. What I was referring to was the United States."

"Why would I do that?"

"Well, if you're going to travel, and make a place in this new world, it's the best way. Otherwise, you're going to have to keep hiding, and I'm not saying it will be easy either way, but it will make it easier if you become a US citizen."

"Oh, well, I'm not sure about that. I don't know what my grandfather would think about that."

"Right, I understand. It's just an idea. We're all citizens."

"Don't you feel hate towards the white man?" Panther asked in a very straight forward manner.

"I did, but I let it go. Hate was eating at my heart, and making me less than human."

"Oh, right."

"I was able to change my mind about many things when I met my wife's father. He enlisted in the U.S. military, not knowing what he was getting into, and soon after he was forced into a war, a war he wanted nothing to do with. But he had to fight or die. While he was in service, he showed great compassion and kindness to the Native American people. And then once he was out, he committed his life to helping our people. He was a very great man."

"Is he gone?" Panther asked as Anna's mom placed a piece of pie in front of him.

"He is, but he watches over us, along with my father, and grandfather. Where is your father?"

"He is gone, he died, and my mother too," he said, and Anna's father looked at him with great empathy.

"Oh, I see."

"This is pie?" Panther said as he stared at the triangle in front of him.

"Yep, blueberry, try a bite, you'll love it," Anna said with a smile, and he did. Loving every second it sat on his tongue.

"Oh, yeah, that's good," he said with a smile, something he hadn't done in quite a long time. He ate his slice of pie and then thanked the kind family for their hospitality. Seeing that their daughter fancied Panther in the Sun, they invited him to stay in the guest bedroom for a few nights, if he would like. He gracefully declined, but having a great fancy for their daughter himself, he stayed close by, sleeping in the neighboring woods, so that he could see her again. He slept by the lake where the star had fallen, pondering what his next move was going to be. Anna went out one night, after everyone was asleep, to find Panther.

"So, you know, you can't stay out here in the woods forever, right?" Anna said as they sat by the starlit water.

"Why not? There's fish in the water, berries in the woods, and well, I have everything I need."

"I guess you're right. But don't you want to have a family and see the world?"

"Yes, I suppose I do."

"Well, you can't do that in the woods, can you?"

"My people have lived off of the goodness of the land forever, of course I can," he said with great pride. "Before they killed every last buffalo, my people, our people, hunted with respect, and then the white man took all that we had, only giving us disease. My people aren't farmers, and even if we were, we can't farm in the dust. I am going to take back what was taken from our people."

"They'll kill you if they feel like it, Panther. Hiding in the woods is not going to work forever. If you face them, as the man that you are, then they will see you are not afraid, and then you can take back what is rightfully yours."

"Well, I guess. I have a notion to leave the United States, and return to the place where my people came from in the first."

"Where would that be?"

"I don't know, but it must be far from here."

"What about love? Would you stay for love?"

"I would always stay for love, and kill for it, too," he said with intensity in his eyes.

"What if I were to say that I was falling in love," Anna said as she looked at the man before her.

"Well," he said and lost his words.

"I could love you," she said and moved closer to him, and leaned in to kiss him.

"I, um, I don't know," he said and backed away. "I hardly know you."

"Yes, I know, but that could change. I'll come to you every day and night, until you see that I'm the woman you will love forever," she said and then quickly kissed him on the cheek, and then ran back home. And, like she said, she returned to him night after night, and soon they fell deeply in love.

"I love your freckle patch," Panther said with a smile as Anna laid with him on a blanket under a sky full of stars. He tenderly kissed the freckles on her cheek. She smiled.

"What else?" she said playfully.

"Let's see," he said as he quickly rolled over on top of her, holding himself up with his arms. "Your lips," he said with a twinkle in his eyes and kissed her softly.

"And," she said while looking into his eyes and caressing his face.

"Your mole," he said with a restrained grin.

"What!" She pinched his cheek firmly with a smile. "I don't have a mole!"

"Ow! No, I said SOUL! You should really get your hearing checked. Speaking of which," he said with a smile as he gently kissed her ear and then her neck. She let out a sigh of pleasure as she turned her head to expose her neck even more.

"I love you," Panther whispered as he lifted his lips from her.

"I love you too," Anna whispered back. Panther laid back down and opened his arm for Anna to snuggle into. They fell asleep in each other's arms that night without a care in the world.

Before long Panther and Anna were ready to move on. So, through the blessing of her father, they had a small Sioux ceremony in their backyard, followed by Panther's citizenship, and a formal American ceremony to document their union. He had never planned these things, but when he found his place in Anna's heart, they naturally became part of the plan. Anna's father insisted that they stay for a while, having secured a job for Panther at his factory workplace. He kindly thanked her father, but declined his offer. He wanted to make it on his own two feet, and her father respected his decision. They traveled back out west, to South Dakota, to find that Eagle's Claw was dying.

"Grandfather, this is my wife, Anna," he said as he knelt by his bedside.

"Anna, let me look at you," he said having to strain, and with great weakness in his voice. Anna knelt down by his side, and he looked into her eyes and held her face. "Oh, yes, she's beautiful," he said. "Panther in the Sun, you are a good man, and I am proud of you," he said as he looked him in the eyes. "It is time for me to go now, but I won't be far. I love you," he said and then laid his head back onto his bed, breathing his last breath.

"Grandfather, wait, not yet!" Panther called out to his leaving spirit and grabbed ahold of his face. "Not yet!" he cried out in tears, then laid his head on his chest. Panther, Anna, and the village buried Eagle's Claw in Sioux fashion, and then moved on. They mourned his loss, celebrated his life, and held him close in their hearts as he parted for the land of the ancestors, where the buffalo still ran.

Panther and Anna continued their westward track until they found the plains of the Rocky Mountains. They kept to themselves, avoiding trouble by avoiding towns. They traveled into what was thought no man's land, and started a life of their own at the base of a great mountain, with a strong creek rushing by. It was spring, and they got busy building a home. They had nothing, other than the supplies that they could wear on their backs, and the small amount of money he earned helping Anna's father on his construction jobs in the few months he lived in Illinois. He built a small shelter for him and Anna to live in, far from anyone, hidden in the trees and started to build a cabin, like the ones he had seen time and time again. By the end of summer, he had built a one room cabin for them to start a family. They lived completely off of the land, taking game with the rifle his father-in-law gave him, fishing in the river, planting crops by the creek side, and foraging for wild edibles. They were well prepared for the winter to come, and settled in for the next four months.

"We've done it," Panther said with a smile as he stoked the fire inside their cabin.

"We sure have," Anna responded as she walked towards Panther rubbing her five-month pregnant belly. She rested her head on Panther's chest and he held her gently. Tears began to well in Anna's eyes as she lifted her head to look up at her husband.

"What's wrong?" Panther asked sweetly as a few tears rolled down Anna's cheek.

"I'm o.k.", she said as she rested her head back on his chest.

"You know you can tell me anything. That hasn't changed," Panther said as he rubbed her back.

"I know."

"So, what's on your mind and in your heart," he asked as he continued to hold her. Anna was silent for a minute or two. Then spoke.

"I'm scared."

"I know. Me too," Panther responded without hesitation.

"You are?" Anna asked with surprise. She gently backed up a step and looked at Panther.

"Yes," of course.

"Well, that's not good. You're never scared. How can we both be scared? You're not supposed to be scared. If you're scared than we aren't going to make it," she said with a panic in her voice.

"I'm scared, but not frightened," Panther responded calmly.

"What? What's the difference? I mean, look at us, we are pregnant in the middle of nowhere. I don't know how to be a mother. What's the future going to look like for our children?" she said with increasing anxiety.

"I understand how you feel. But, I promise you this. What you're feeling is normal and actually good," Panther said, keeping his emotions in check.

"Good? It surely doesn't feel good," Anna snapped back.

"Moments of fear are good. It forces us to look at ourselves, search within, reach out to one another and reach out to God," Panther said as he stepped closer to Anna and took her hands. "You are the strongest woman I have ever known. You've been a source of strength for me, just as much as I have been for you. This moment of fear will pass just as fast as it rose. Just so long as you face it and claim who you are. You are strength and love," Panther said with deep sincerity as he took in the entirety of the love of his life, standing before him. "You already are the best mother." Anna searched Panther's eyes and then returned to his arms. She held Panther just as he held her. They didn't exchange anymore words. They just held each other in peace as the fire blazed, popped and threw off warmth as the winter wind whipped outside.

Spring came, and they emerged from their cabin nine months pregnant. Anna gave birth to a beautiful baby boy, and they couldn't have been happier.

"We should name him after your grandfather, don't you think?" Anna said as she held her baby.

"Well," he said with huge eyes at the sight of his child, breathing, and there, with them. "I'm not sure, that's not really a baby's name, and I'm not sure what his baby name was. So, how about, I don't know, let's see," he said as he took his baby into his arms. "How about Lakota," he said and looked into his baby's eyes.

"O.k., I love it," Anna said as she laid her head back on to her pillow. The next two years flew by in a whirlwind of love and joy like they had never known. And just when they thought it couldn't get any better, they gave birth to another baby boy, named Dakota, welcoming him into their circle of love. Life was good, simple, and how Panther always imagined life could be like. They hadn't seen a single soul in years, other than a couple of trappers who just passed by. They had carved out a life in the wild, and were thriving in their environment. The children were strong, happy, and healthy when winter came, at the ages of three and one.

"O.k. Lakota, you help mommy with Dakota, o.k.? I'll be home in just a little while," Panther said and then headed out to hunt, now with his bow. Since being in the wild, he refused buying products, like bullets, especially from the people that destroyed his people. His pride for his own people was at its highest, as he lived a life free of any constraints or dependency. He was young, strong, capable, and had everything he needed in the woods and in his family.

He quietly stalked, then climbed into a tree. He waited for an hour for his prey to come by, a large buck. His eyes scanned the woods with an arrow notched. The deer, not aware of his presence, in sight or smell, moved hesitantly into range. Panther's heart started to pound and adrenaline began to release, as he waited for his moment. The deer moved closer, seemingly staring right at him, and Panther waited. He waited for him to show his flank, then, when the time was right, as the deer looked in the opposite direction, he drew his bow and then let fly a deadly arrow. The arrow struck the deer right in the heart. It stammered a few yards, and then fell. He placed his hands on the deer's body and gave thanks to the Great Spirit and to the deer. He cut two long poles, attached the deer to them, and then dragged his kill home. He walked with a smile for the goodness the deer would bring to his family. As he neared his home, a feeling of unrest came to his spirit. He tried to shrug it off, but it was too real to do so. He cleared the forest line, and was close to his home when the feeling overwhelmed him. He dropped the deer, then he, himself, dropped to the ground. He looked up from the snow and dead grass in stalking fashion, saw a white man standing at his front door armed with a rifle. He kept low, and sprinted to the back entrance.

He armed himself with his hatchet, and then stormed into his home, where his fear became reality as his wife lay naked, bleeding on the floor with a man standing over her, getting ready to go for the children. He rushed at the man, and split his head in half with the hatchet as rage beyond the depth of hell rushed through his body. He quickly scanned the room, and found his children whimpering in the corner. He then rushed to the front, kicked open the door, and found the other man running, trying to shoot as he went, firing wildly passed Panther. He was well out of his reach, so Panther stopped, and ran back to his children and dying wife. He grabbed his children, told them it was o.k., set them in bed, and then rushed to his wife.

"Anna!" he cried as he lifted her head, feeling the blood poor from the back of her skull. "Oh God, No!" he yelled as he tore off his shirt, and wrapped her head in vain.

"You," she struggled to speak as her eyes began to roll back. "Must go, with children," she was able to get out with great struggle. "Now!" she gasped, and then died.

"Anna! No! Don't leave me! Don't leave your children!" he screamed as he held her lifeless body. He held her in tears for a minute, then her words echoed in his soul, as he ran for a blanket, and covered her body. He dressed his children in their winter coats, and then he grabbed her baby back pack, picked up Dakota, kissed his cheek, put him in the pack and carried Lakota in his arm. He grabbed his rifle and emergency rounds, some food, and a pouch of water, then ran. He knew the white men would return, in numbers and armed. They would kill him, and the children. He ran like he had never run before, straight to the woods, and towards the mountains. His heart was racing, and his mind too. His only concern was for his children, as he ran even faster straight to the base of the mountains. He stopped, looked up at the immensity of the mountains, and then looked back in the direction of the inevitable man hunt that was about to ensue.

"Daddy, I'm scared," Lakota said as he felt his father starting to tremble. He tried to ease his fear, but he was screaming on the inside. He looked down to the ground, seeing his footsteps the entire way back. They were sure to find him, especially with them coming on horseback, and they would surely kill him and his children. If he ran, they would freeze to death. He couldn't make a fire, as the smoke would give them away. The winter would kill them. His heart pounded as he started to panic, and the children both began to cry. So, without knowing what else to do, he started to run again. He ran like ten horses, and didn't stop for the next hour. Dakota began to whimper, and Lakota too as he straddled his father's side.

"O.k., o.k.," he said as he set Lakota down next to the tree, and took Dakota from his back, now crying harder, in desperate need of his mother. "It's o.k. baby; it's o.k." he said as he held his baby against his chest and patted his back, trying to calm himself down, so as to calm his child.

"Daddy, I'm thirsty and hungry, so is Dakota," Lakota said as he looked up at his father with pitiful eyes.

"O.k. baby, hang on," he said as he grabbed the little pieces of meat and pouch from the back pack. He gave them both water, which was almost impossible to do, because Dakota was still nursing.

"He wants his milky," Lakota said as he chewed on a piece of dried venison.

"I know baby; it's o.k.," he said as he tried to get him to drink a little bit, but he was refusing.

"He won't eat meat yet either," Lakota said.

"I know," he said with great desperation in his voice and eyes.

"Where's momma?" Lakota asked, and Panther's heart melted and broke at the same time as he looked into his eyes.

"She's gone, baby," he said as he fought back the tears.

"Where did she go?" he asked as Dakota tried in vain to nurse, rooting his little face into his father's chest.

"She's in heaven, she's happy with God," he said, as he put Dakota back into his pack and then strapped him on.

"Why did she leave us, wasn't she happy with us?"

"She was baby, but some bad men took her from us, o.k.? She's dead," he said not knowing what else to say as he picked him up. He knew what he had to do, and that was to turn himself in. He was an American citizen, they would have to give him a fair trial, and his children would live. He ran in the direction of town, only in a roundabout way. He had to make it there before they were hunted down like pigs. He could sense them tracking, and so he picked up his pace. He swerved through the trees, barely sinking his feet into the snow, as if skimming across the surface. The faster he ran, the quieter the children became, so he kept running.

They reached the outskirts of the nearest town, and he kept running. He ran straight into town, ignoring the stares and hearing the pounding of horses on the verge of capturing him. He sprinted into the sheriff's office, and nearly collapsed as he tried to find the right words.

"I, I," he said as he tried to catch his breath.

"Yes, can I help you?" the man with a badge asked behind the desk. He could hear the horses getting closer.

"A man killed my wife, and I killed him in return," he said as he pulled Dakota off his back, and let Lakota stand. He took Dakota out of his pack, and rocked him.

"O.k. . . . sheriff!" the man called to the back room.

"Yeah!" he responded.

"We got a situation," the deputy said as he got up.

"I'm a U.S. citizen, and I know my rights. Please do not harm my children," Panther said as the man moved slowly towards him. At the very same moment the main entrance door flew open, and a man charged in with his rifle, only to be stopped by the now drawn pistol of the sheriff as he rushed from the back.

"Drop it!" the sheriff yelled as Panther tucked Lakota behind him and covered Dakota.

"This Indian killed a white man. Don't point that at me!" the man said not willing to yield.

"Yeah well, this white man's about to kill you, so drop it!" the sheriff yelled and moved closer with his pistol, and the deputy was now drawn as well.

"Alright, alright," the man said, then dropped his weapon.

"Cuff 'em both," the sheriff said.

"Right, get down! Hands on head!" the deputy yelled to the once armed man, and proceeded to cuff him. "You, too, hands behind your back," he said as the sheriff tried to take Dakota from Panther's gripping, unwilling to let go, hands. "Sir, let him go," he said as he gave Panther a reassuring eye. He let him go, and the sheriff took the children behind the desk. The deputy took Panther, and the other man to different cells in the back, locked the doors and left them.

"You inbred piece of crap Indian, this is all your fault!" the man yelled and Panther just slid down the wall, overcome by emotions, and wept. "Yeah, you should cry, you weak heart! Your wife was sexy as all get out. I got to see the whole thing!" Panther's fist clinched as he rose from the cell floor, and ran at the bars screaming. He gripped the cold iron bars, and wailed to the sky.

"He-ay-hee-ee!" he yelled to the Great Spirit. "He-ay-hee-ee!" He yelled in desperation. "Bring me my children! Bring me my children!" he screamed down the corridor in vain, as the large door barricaded all sound.

"Shut up, you stupid ass Indian!" the man called from his cell. Panther wanted to rip his throat out, and tried to reach around to grab a hold of him, but was stopped short by the bars.

2

LAKOTA AND DAKOTA WERE PUT STRAIGHT AWAY INTO THE ORPHAN-
age system. Panther wasn't allowed to see them, not even a goodbye.
He was questioned as to any living relatives, and he gave them Anna's parents as the absolute necessary people his children should go
to. Upon attempting to contact them, there was no answer, nor response. They tried for one day more to contact and locate them, but
they were unable to. So, they officially turned the children over to
social services. It was then that Lakota and Dakota became separated into two different states, due to overcrowding of the orphanages
and they became lost in the system. After further attempts to contact
Anna's parents, a final conclusion was determined as to their status.
They had all burnt to death in a house fire, arson was the determined cause, and officials were still investigating the case. It turned
out that Anna's father was making great strides in the construction
business, making his way up to contractor. This didn't sit well with
a few of the men, and out of an act of blind rage and jealousy, they
torched his house as they slept.

Panther in the Sun had his day in court, as he had hoped, and the
verdict crushed him like he had never expected. His public defender

argued he acted in self-defense, but the prosecution attempted to argue that Panther killed both his wife and the man in a jealous rage. They argued that she was having an affair, and the man standing watch attested to this lie. In front of God and with his hand on the Bible, he claimed that she consented and that it was his duty to make sure that her husband didn't show up and kill them both. Panther's defense was able to disprove this theory by the autopsy reports that displayed forceful vaginal entry. The jury showed mercy on Panther, but not to the extent of self-defense. They charged him with murder in the second degree, and sentenced him to twenty-five years in the Colorado State Penitentiary. The man who stood watch was charged with accessory to murder, and was charged with ten years.

All the while, the suffering began for the now orphaned boys. "Damn it, I have enough to do, you do it for once," the disgruntled, exhausted orphanage care worker woman said as she ignored the cries of Dakota, who was now given the name "Charlie", in the Boulder County Orphanage. Dakota cried for the next two hours before they finally got around to changing his diaper, and feeding him.

"I swear, I'd rather be doing anything else right now," another woman said as she laid a bottle next to Dakota in a crib of three babies.

"Then why don't you," still another lady said in the crowded room full of babies. "We don't need your negativity around here."

"O.k. Mrs. goody two shoes, thank God most of us are like me. You make me sick."

"Why do you even work here? These are humans, if you haven't looked around," the kinder lady spoke as she picked up a baby and burped her.

"It's called community service," she said, as she changed a diaper with a look of disgust.

"Dear God, have mercy on these children," the woman said.

Meanwhile in a small county of Nebraska, Lakota (who was given the name "John") was also fighting for survival.

"I have a daddy," he said as he and a mass of other children played in the orphanage commons.

"No you don't; nobody has a daddy here," the jaded six-year old said and pushed Lakota.

"Hey!" he yelled and kicked the kid in the shin.

"Ow, you little puke!" the kid yelled and then smacked Lakota, sending him to the ground.

"Hey, hey, that's enough, both of you!" An old, grey haired lady yelled behind her spectacles as she held two babies, both now crying. "Both to the corner! Now!" she yelled as she kicked them along into opposite corners for the next hour. "Anyone else want to act up or fight, huh? It'll be the discipline room, next, I swear to God!" she yelled at the mass of kids. The discipline room was a small room with a bucket for a toilet where a child was left isolated for two days without any interaction with anyone. They would open the door, push a plate of slop in, and lock it back. Once you turned three you were old enough to go there. Lakota cried quietly in the corner, so as not to be heard, because outwardly crying was punishable, and he dreaded the idea of the discipline room. Memories of his momma holding him flashed into his head, and his daddy tickling him, as he cried with his face in the corner. He held on to the hope that his daddy would come for him, and that he still loved him. And that his momma would wake up and bring him home.

A fiery burst from hell had overtaken Panther in the Sun's family. In a blink of an eye he lost all that mattered to him, and he was struggling to stay alive. In his prison cell, every breath he took was laborious, and in the first year there wasn't a moment that he didn't want to kill himself. The pain was unbearable, unimaginable, and overwhelming to his soul. He sat up late that night, and as always thought of his children. The thoughts always led to tears, and he fought the temptation to stop all of the memories, and stop all of the praying, and stop all of the worrying. He wanted to shake the pain, so that he could stay alive for his children. So, instead of erasing the emotion, he used it as fuel.

"Hey, pass me that soap," a man said next to him in the showers.

"Use your own," Panther said as he tried to ignore the man.

"What? You feathered bastard, pass me the soap," he said and then another man moved in.

"Alright, take it easy," he said as he handed over the soap.

"There you go, that's more like it. Now, let's see," the man said as he pretended to turn back around into his own shower, but then quickly swung around and punched Panther in the jaw, knocking him back. The other man jumped in, and he was unable to escape. He was half their size, and they easily overpowered him, raping him and taking every last ounce of dignity that he had tried to retain.

He wept in his cell that night, but found surprising comfort in the man he shared the cell with.

"Hey, hey man, you o.k.?" he asked as he looked down from the top bunk.

"No," he said from the depths of his own hell.

"Hey man, you know there's light at the end of the tunnel, right?" the powerful, large black man said as he climbed down.

30

"I don't think so, not for me," Panther said now fighting back more tears.

"Hey man, I used to feel that way too, about ten years ago. It gets better, I mean not better, but some of the pain goes away."

"This pain will never go away!" he said with bubbling snot and ferocity in his eyes.

"O.k. man, o.k. You know what, we all need friends in here, and I'm willing to be that guy," he said with sincerity. "I know what happened to you man, all of it. Including tonight. Hey, from now on, when you go out, we go out. You hang with me and my guys now. O.k.?"

"Yeah, o.k.," Panther said as some weight was removed from him. He went to sleep that night, feeling better that not everyone wanted to rape him. He woke in the morning to the guards rattling their cages.

"Stick with me, Sun," his roommate Terrel said, as he hopped down from his bunk.

"Yeah, o.k., thanks," Panther said as he got up, peed in their toilet, and brushed his teeth alongside of Terrel, the man who hadn't said one word for the last two weeks, since he became his new cellmate.

"You're gonna be alright, man," Terrel said with a mouth full of toothpaste, and then spit into the sink, having to lean down about two feet so as not to miss.

"Yeah, o.k." Panther said as he felt empowered by the protection that his new-found friend was offering. He thought of his children, and their images strengthened him to do whatever he could to survive prison, and see them on the other side. He had no idea where they were, as his letter to social services was responded with indecision. They informed him of the national overload, and that his children were split apart. And, in all reality, the records were basically non-existent due to the amount of orphaned children. So, all he knew was that his children weren't together. His vision of Dakota being soothed by his older brother was no longer a source of hope, and now he had nothing to hold on to, nor did his children.

"Just keep running. That'll make it better. Run faster, jump . . . breathe, breathe deeper . . . where could he be? Why isn't he coming for me?" John, only eleven years old, thought as he ran to forget. He ran until he got to his traps down by the creek side, bought with his own hard-earned money and found them empty. "Why hasn't he come for me?" The distant thought of his father alive and calling his name haunted the boy as he ran back to his foster home in Nebraska, dreading the night.

"Where have you been boy?" his foster parent asked, not knowing the boy had been trapping to make money of his own.

"I was running, that's all," John said and tried to walk by.

"Don't be wasting energy boy, unless you're working for me," he said as he grabbed the boy's arm, keeping him from passing.

"O.k." he said timidly with his shaved head hung low.

"What?" he said as he grabbed him tighter and pulled him in front of him.

"I mean, yes sir," the boy said with fear in his brown, soulful eyes.

"Alright," the man said and then released his grip. "Now come on, we're getting dinner."

They walked over to the barn, and the man pointed to a cow, ready to be taken.

"Alright boy, do it," the man said as he handed him the rifle.

"No, I'd rather you," he stammered, looking at a cow he had come to know. He milked her and twenty others every morning at four a.m. for the last two years.

"What'd you say?" he said with mean eyes. "Do it."

"Alright, alright," he said and took the rifle. He thought about shooting the man instead, and wished that he could. He envisioned it in his mind, and smiled on the inside.

"Well, what you waitin' on?"

"Nothin'," he said as he envisioned the cow as the man, and then lifted the heavy rifle with surprising ease for his lean body. He pulled the trigger quickly. Blast! Right in the head.

"Good, now were talkin'," the man said and snatched the gun back from the boy. "You get busy making steaks boy. Don't foul up. I'll be back to make sure you ain't. And clean up all the blood, too, I don't want no damn mess in here."

"That's why we should do it in the field," the boy said as he started to make a long cut into the gut.

"What?" the man said as he rushed at the boy and kicked him in the side, knocking him into the bloody cow.

"Nothin', sorry," he said and covered his head from further attack.

"Right, get to work, damn it."

"He means well, John, I know it's hard to see that," Mrs. Forester said as she set the plates alongside of her foster son.

"No he doesn't, and you know it," he said quietly so as not to be heard. "He wouldn't push me around, or make me do his dirty work if he did."

"Now you watch your tone young man," she said and gave him a look that clearly displayed that John should be grateful. "He puts this roof over your head, so you just watch it."

"Yeah, I guess," he said as he continued to set the table.

"Hey, mom," Susan, the oldest girl said, as she entered the dining room. "John," she said with indifference.

"Hey Susan, wash up for dinner, we're having ribeye steaks tonight," she said with a smile for her daughter, as John left the room and went in to wash up.

"How's your day, Susan?" John said as he stood patiently waiting to wash his hands.

"Wouldn't you like to know," she said sarcastically as she looked at herself in the mirror.

"Yeah, I would," he said.

"I don't want to waste my breath."

"O.k., good, because I don't want to smell it," he said and then stuck his tongue out at her.

"What did you say? Mom!" she yelled, and then stormed out to tell.

"Hey, wait, I was just kidding," John said and tried to stop her from telling, but it was too late. She went straight to her mom, and unfortunately her dad was right there, too.

"What did you say to her?" Mr. Forester said as he started to undo his belt.

"He said she had bad breath," Mrs. Forester said with her arms folded standing next to her daughter, encouraging the beating.

"I'm sorry, I'm sorry!" John cried, but it was useless. He was dragged into the guest bedroom, his room, and beaten until his back started to bleed.

"Now you think about what you did wrong, and I don't want to see you until you get back from school and are ready to work," he said and the slammed the door. John cried himself to sleep that night, gripping his pillow praying that his father would come for him.

At the same time, on a farm in Arkansas, a nine-year-old Charlie fought for what little dignity he had in him.

"You stupid orphan, I'm gonna whip your Injun ass like your daddy wishes he could do," the twelve-year old kid said as he pushed Charlie from behind, as he tried to walk away, but was met with great resistance as Charlie was sturdy and strong.

"My daddy would whoop your ass, and your daddy's!" Charlie yelled with pain behind his brownish-green eyes as he turned back around and charged the much bigger kid, the neighbor to his foster parent's home.

"Ha, ha," he laughed as he jumped out of the way, letting Charlie fall to the ground. He quickly rose, and rushed again, this time connecting a flying kick to the side of the kid's knee, buckling it and sending him to the ground. "AAAAHHHH!" the kid screamed as he rolled around in the dirt. "You little terd! AAAAHHHH!" he screamed again in front of a small crowd of kids, and Charlie ran for his life. He knew he couldn't go back to his home, fearing the whipping of a lifetime, so he just kept running. He ran into the woods, stayed there all night, and went to school in the morning, where he was confronted by his principal.

"Now, Charlie, you can't keep fighting everyone. I received a call from your foster parents, and they want you to come home, o.k.?" the kind but stern man said from behind the desk.

"Why, so they can whip me?" he said behind teary eyes.

"Well, you really hurt that boy, so I don't know what they're going to do. But if they really hurt you, you tell me, and I'll do something about it. o.k.?"

"Alright. Why don't I have any parents? Are they dead? Where are they?"

"I'm not sure, Charlie," he lied, knowing full well the situation. "But, if things don't work out for you over there, then we'll move you to a better home. o.k.?"

"O.k."

"Good boy, you run along now. Hey, if you study hard, you can be anything you want to be, and that's what matters right now."

"Yes, sir," he said and went back to his classroom where he spent the entire day daydreaming about what it would be like to have a real family, a family that loved him.

Later that day, Charlie faced punishment for defending himself from a bully.

"Our son is lying in a hospitable bed because of what your miserable little bastard child did," the bully's mom said outside of the Johnson's door.

The Johnson's were Charlie's foster parents. His stay with them had been quite lengthy and very emotionally damaging to Charlie.

"We're very sorry, right Charlie?" Mrs. Johnson said as she looked down at Charlie.

"I am sorry, very sorry," he said sincerely as he looked up at both of the women.

"Yeah, well you should be. The doctor said he tore a ligament in his knee, and that it won't heal for a very long time. He's going to have to wear a brace just to walk, thanks to you. You're lucky you're not in juvenile hall, and we could sue the pants off of you people. You're lucky we're good people, dear God," she said and grabbed her forehead.

"Don't worry, he's going to be punished, you can believe that Mrs. Connors."

"Yes, well, good," she said and then walked away.

"Upstairs Charlie," Mrs. Johnson said as she pointed to the stairs.

"O.k.," he said as he hung his head and walked up. "What are you going to do to me?"

"I don't know, Charlie, I have to wait for Mr. Johnson to get home, then we'll decide. You stay in here until then," she said sternly and closed the door behind her. When Mr. Johnson did get home, he entered into Charlie's room with his belt in hand. He had a look of anger, and for some reason or another, turned into a look of remorse. He sat Charlie on the bed and broke the news.

"Charlie, well I wish I could just whip you and get it over with, but, well, I don't know how to tell you this, but . . . well, we're not able to keep you here no more. You'll be going back to the orphanage until they can find you another home," he said as he looked into his searching eyes.

"Why?" Charlie asked.

"Well, it's just not going to work out. Don't worry, you'll find your place, and maybe someday you'll find your dad. So, Mrs. Johnson will help you get your things together, and see you off tomorrow morning. Hey . . . don't you forget about our secret. If you tell anyone, we'll find out, and well . . . let's just say you'll never be the same again," he said as he stood up and left.

"Right," Charlie said with his head hung low. Charlie returned to the orphanage the very next day.

The never-ending struggle continued for Panther as he paced the yard, just as he always did for the last eight years, plotting an escape that he knew he would never follow through with. If he tried to escape, without success, he would definitely have time added to his already too-long sentence. And if he did successfully escape, which he fantasized about doing, he would have to kidnap his own children. They would be on the run with them; that's if he could even find them. He found that his energy was going in the wrong direction, and so he had to finally come to some sort of terms. Terms that would enable a level of peace, even though he found that to be impossible in his situation. He would have to be on his best behavior, do anything possible to cut down his time, and wait it out.

"Man, c'mon, it's work time." Terrel tapped Panther with the back of his hand as Panther stared off into nowhere, impervious of the call for the chain gang. They quickly got into line, and went off to work.

John woke early that morning, as he always did, and made his way down to the cows. He hand milked all twenty of them every day, without fail. He got so good at it that he could literally do it in a half -sleep state, in order to save energy for the long day ahead. After he milked the cows, it was straight to the chickens, where he fed, collected eggs, and scooped chicken poop for fertilizer. Then it was on to the pigs, whom he knew by name. He fed them their slop, and then moved to the large garden to spread the chicken poo. All of this before six o'clock a.m., at which time he took his bath in a creek, then ate breakfast with the family. He made his own lunch for the day, consisting of a piece of bread dipped in lard, and an apple, then was off to school. He waited by the bus stop, and then got aboard.

"Lookie, lookie, the Indian bastard," a red headed bully said as John walked down the aisle of the bus.

"Shut up, Jasper, you're just jealous," a kind girl, John's friend, said.

"OOH, you like the Indian, ha ha! You guys should get married and have little half-breed retards!"

"Yeah, ha ha!" another kid chimed. John ignored them, and sat next to the girl.

"Thanks," John said.

"Don't mention it," she said and then looked out the window. "He really is jealous. You're the fastest kid in the school, and maybe the smartest."

"Oh, thanks," John said as he looked down at his used, worn shoes, and looked at his calloused hands.

"You're the nicest boy I know," she said with kind eyes for John.

"Thank you, you're pretty nice too."

John went to school that day, and studied harder than anyone in the school. He went above and beyond every day, and was a favorite among the teachers.

"John, you keep it up, and you can do whatever you want with your future," his science teacher said after class.

"Yes sir, thank you, sir."

"John, how are things at home?"

"It's o.k., it could be better."

"Yeah, well, you hang in there, and keep working hard in school. Also athletics will serve you well too, so stick with those too. You sure can run."

"Yes sir, well, I have to get to my next class. Thank you."

"You're welcome."

John went home that late afternoon after cross country practice, and found a house in distress. Mr. Forester had been drinking all day, ignoring any and all of his responsibilities, which he more than often put onto John, and was in a drunken rage.

"There he is, my miserable, good for nothing, Indian slave! How about you show me how tough you are, you little bastard," he said as the girls stood paralyzed and helpless in the corner of the living room.

"No thank you, sir, I'd rather go about doing my chores, if you don't mind."

"No, no, I want to see how tough you are. I think Indians ain't nothing but cowards," he said and gave John a taunting look. Something stirred in John like never before, and the pride of his people began to rise in his body. "C'mon, let's do this! Here, hit me, right here," Mr. Forester said wobbling as he stuck out his chin. John thought about it, and then a power like he had never known rose, and he felt the power surge from his feet, all the way into his fist and he struck him with every last bit of strength that he had. The drunken fool fell to the ground.

"You little bastard, what the hell? Did you see what he just did?" he said as he grabbed his jaw, struggling to talk.

"You asked for it daddy," his daughter said.

"What'd you say?" he said and then started for her. She ran from him as he stumbled after her, looking to release his anger. He nearly caught up to her, when Mrs. Forester took a lamp and smashed it over his head. He fell to the ground, bleeding profusely from the wound, and that's when Mrs. Forester called the operator to get the police out to their address. Mr. Forester got up, ran in a wobbly manner to the back room, got his shotgun, and came back out in a drunken fury. Everyone ran out into the twilight, and scattered as he began firing wild shots. He was able to single out John, and raised his gun to shoot. Just as he was about to fire, he tripped on a log, his knee knocked the butt end of the gun, sending the barrel towards his own throat, and that's when he fell, pulling the trigger as he dropped, and blew his own head off.

The police arrived, and Mrs. Forester, as well as her daughter attested to the sequence of events, and it was deemed a fatal accident. It was at this point, the Forester's decided that it would be best that John return to the orphanage, in hopes of him finding a more suitable family. John packed his few possessions, and returned to the orphanage the very next day.

The days, weeks, months and years had dragged on with ceaseless monotony. Wake, work, sleep, much like most of the world only without the welcomed interruptions of love, play, and freedom. Panther, known as prisoner number 6809, and "Sun" to most, was becoming numb. The memories he held so tight were beginning to fade as the institutionalization set in. He fought every night as he layed in bed to remember. He willed the preservation, as hard as it was, and would go through a ritual of thoughts before he went to sleep. He would start from his very first memory, a vision of the bright sun lighting the face of his mother as they walked in a field of wildflowers, and this would lead into his father holding him by the fire light, as his people danced late into the night. His next thought was his grandfather showing him the way of animal tracks, and sharing a smile. He then thought of Anna, her beautiful smile, and the first time they met. He quietly spoke to her as he lay, and then moved on to his favorite memories. He thought of holding Lakota as he slept, feeling his little heart beating against his own, and how he swore he would never let anything come in between them. He thought of his first steps and his little smiles. Then he would think of the same exact love for Dakota, as he rested against his daddy's chest.

Panther woke the next morning to another day of hard labor and monotony.

"Another day in paradise," Terrel said as he hopped down from the bunk.

"Yep, another day."

"Hey, I've got something I need to talk to you about. We'll talk later tonight. Don't forget to remind me, o.k.?" Terrel said with great seriousness in his voice.

"Alright."

"Also, I talked to Red, and he's willing to start training you, if you want."

"Really, that's great," Panther said while sitting on the toilet, and Terrel brushed his teeth.

"He thinks you have great potential. He doesn't do this for just anyone, so it's a real honor. That old dude's the baddest guy in here, heavy weight champ, three years in a row."

"Yeah, that's great. Why me?"

"Cause I asked him, man, that's why. You were the one talking about wanting to do it, remember?"

"Yeah, I do."

"Well good, c'mon, dang, light a match or something, that's some nasty stuff boy!"

"Sorry, prison food."

It wasn't too long before Charlie's and John's lives would finally take a turn for the better. They were placed in new foster homes that would soon become their new adopted families. Charlie was taken on by a kind Christian family, the Morrison's, and John by a kind Jewish family named the Rosenthal's. The years of neglect and abuse had finally come to an end, as each family treated the children with kindness and respect. John was now sixteen years old, and thriving in his new environment in his Chicago home. His foster father was an honest businessman, his foster mother a practicing nurse. Their own children were fully grown by the time John came into their life at the age of twelve. John was excelling in academics, athletics, and as a result was finding it quite easy to make friends at his high school.

Charlie was also living a life deserved. He was fourteen, and a freshman in high school. His foster parents were kind-hearted people, with sincere care, and interest in Charlie's life. His foster parents had three children of their own, a boy, eleven, a girl, fifteen, and another boy, eighteen and on his own. Like John, Charlie was thriving in his new environment, making new friends, and excelling in his school work, as well as athletics. He had just started to learn the piano, as well. His life in Kansas was a far cry from the life he had known previous. But, like John, the major pieces of his heart were missing, and they were both struggling internally to find their true places. But the kindness shown to them was enough to keep them going and striving for more. Each of them held on to the hope that someday their father would come for them. They were told the truth about their mother, but were continually given mixed information about their father. Everybody involved was trying to protect them from the false hope of his return, as his sentence would extend well into their adult lives. This was what social services told their foster families to perpetuate, as well. But through all of the misinformation, the boys knew the truth. Their father was going to be in prison for a very long time but would one day be free. And as far as the boys were concerned, they were only children. When Lakota, "John", would have a memory of a little brother, it would always be dismissed as a false childhood memory. But, again, he knew in his heart of hearts the truth.

Charlie's freshman year was a year of outstanding accomplishments and record-breaking athletic achievement. Not only was he the anchor on the varsity relay team, he was also the starting guard on the basketball team, and great hopeful on the cross country team. Both boys could run like the wind. Charlie's freshman athletic achievement was being mirrored by John in his Junior year. He already had colleges looking at him for his athletic prowess, as well as his academic excellence. That fall, both Charlie and John were the cross country champions of their respective states. John in Illinois, and Charlie in Kansas. These states just so happened to have what John and Charlie needed after their abusive situations-quality foster homes. What was to follow was an epic race that would boggle the minds of anyone in the sports world. It was the regional championships, and in the competition was Iowa, Illinois, Indiana, Ohio, Michigan, Wisconsin, Kentucky, and Kansas.

"I sure am nervous," Charlie said as he rode in the back seat of the car to Indiana.

"You're going to be great," Charlie's brother by adoption, Jack, said.

"Thanks, Jack."

"I hope I can run like you when I get older."

"You will, don't worry about that."

"Jack's right, you're going to be great," Mr. Morrison said with a smile into his rear view mirror.

"Thanks."

"You just give it your all, and you'll be fine," Mrs. Morrison said as she turned her head back.

"Just break wind when someone's behind you; that'll help," Kelly, the fifteen-year old suggested with a laugh.

"Kelly!"

"It's not a bad idea," Mr. Morrison said with a smile.

"Rick! You guys are so bad!"

Meanwhile, Mr. Rosenthal drove John to Indiana to make the race as well.

"I hear there's this kid from Kansas, a freshman, who's incredible," John said to his foster dad as he sat in the front seat. It was just the two of them.

"Yeah, I heard of him. Pretty amazing. You got 'im though," he said and gave him a little smile.

"I don't know, but what I do know is that there's gonna be a lot of good runners there, and that's fine by me."

"Good attitude." Mr. Rosenthal said while nodding his head.

"Yeah. I can't wait for college. Which college do you think is better, University of Ilinois or DePaul?"

"Honestly?"

"Of course."

"Either one is fantastic. We're very proud of you, and we'll miss you when you're gone."

"Yeah, you guys have been really good to me, and you didn't even have to."

"Well, the way I look at it is that we're all in this together, no matter what race, religion, family situation, whatever. When someone needs help, you give it to them."

"I wish my mom and dad were here to see me race."

"I wish they were too. You know there is no one on the face of the planet that can love you like your own parents, and you know what? That love is right there in your heart. You were loved like nothing or no one ever, and that love is still in you, so don't you worry about that, o.k.?"

"Yeah, I guess you're right."

Sun had become a formidable fighting machine. He trained with a world champion boxer for years on end, and had become a limber rock of a man. The warden himself was so impressed with his ability, after several arranged fights, that he had a ring built in the yard, just for boxing. He bought the men gloves, and instead of the usual tension, and out of control fights, involving crude weapons, much of the aggression was released in the ring. And on top of his weight class was "Panther," the name used for when Sun was in the ring. He knocked every last opponent out in the Colorado State Pen and now the warden was arranging fights with other prisons, gambling on each and every one of them. Panther saw it as a good chance to save up some money for when he got out, and the warden also promised to knock off some time if he produced some wins. So, Panther trained harder than ever. He had served thirteen years of a twenty-five year sentence, and if he kept winning, he'd be out in three or four years.

His first inter-penitentiary bout came quicker than he'd planned. The warden was raring to go, ready to cash in on Panthers' talents in the ring. And talented he was. He was quicker than anyone, and just as soon as the opponent thought they were going to land a punch, they were taking one in the gut or head. His moves soon became coined the "Panther's Flash," and when he hit, he hit with a strength that was uncanny. The stage was set, and they bussed his six foot-three, two-hundred and ten-pound black opponent in, as well as his trainer, the warden and a few privileged inmates. His name was "Ruthless" and was the best fighter at the federal penitentiary in the upper state of Colorado. He was, by all accounts, as his namesake plainly stated, ruthless. The inmates were like caged monkeys, hooting and howling with the excitement of the nearing event.

"Alright fellas, I want a clean fight, no bitin', kickin', rabbit punchin', nothing below the belt, got it?"

"Yeah," Panther replied, and "Ruthless" just nodded.

"Now shake and let's get this goin'," the hired referee said, backed away, and the bell rang on the outdoor ring. The sun blazed mid-summer heat, and the fight began. Panther danced around the ring, drawing his opponent in, then covered, got low, then exploded shots to the ribs. Ruthless, all power, swung wildly at his head, but it was easily avoided by a duck, and then a counter-punch to the body. Ruthless cringed, and bent with the blow, then quickly moved back. Panther moved in again, throwing a missed hook, that threw him off balance. Ruthless took advantage, and struck him with a left blow to the side of his head. Panther was already teetering, and the shot sent him to the floor. He went black for a count of two, then heard the referee.

"Three, four." Panther pushed himself up, and avoided another shot. The bell rang, and the men went to their corners.

At the same time, over in Indiana, his boys were about to face off in a race of a lifetime, one in which they were competing against one another, yet had no clue that they were doing so. Charlie's coach was giving him the race strategy, one in which he was to pace himself, then in the last mile, of the three and a half-mile race, he was to make his move. Charlie nodded, and looked to his teammates who were all antsy to start the race. He then looked over to the regional favorite, the junior from Illinois. He sized him up, looking him up and down from afar, and then concentrated on getting loose for the race. Within the next few minutes thirty runners took their marks on a country course that weaved in between trees, crossed a bridge, and then circled back to a dirt road that finally lead to the home stretch in an open field where the race was to begin. The path was lined with markers, and set to accommodate the finest young runners in the country.

"Runners, take your marks, get set, BANG!" the blast from the starter's pistol boomed and the runners took off. Charlie forgot the game plan as he sprinted to the front of the pack, setting the pace, and holding the lead.

"Charlie!" his coach screamed, but he was deaf to the call. John wondered what the heck this kid was doing, his pace was insanely fast, and he figured that it was part of their game plan as he stayed in the middle of the pack. He assumed he was playing the rabbit role, to wear out the opposing runners, and then make room for his teammates to steadily take the race. Two miles passed, and Charlie was still leading the race.

"I can't keep this up," Charlie thought as he sprinted along. "Oh my God, this is crazy," he thought again. "I can't let anyone pass me. Keep going, keep going," he told himself as he concentrated on his breathing, two breaths in, one out. Two breaths in, one out.

"What is this kid doing? That's it, I'm making my move," John said to himself, and picked up his pace considerably, moving into fourth place. He kept his position, and there was only three quarters of a mile left to go. Charlie, amazingly, and unfathomably, picked up his pace, distancing himself even further from the pack. John took off after him. He ran to within fifty yards of him, and left the rest of the pack behind. It was just the two of them, a freshman from Kansas, and a junior from Illinois. Charlie's skinny frame flew across the field, nearing the final stretch. The crowd started to yell even louder, cheering for both racers. John closed the gap, with only two hundred yards to go, and Charlie started to weaken. His face clinched, and muscles started to spasm. His breath was no longer in rhythm, and John pulled up equal to him. Just when they thought they were the only ones in the final stretch, they heard the hooves and heavy breathing of another runner. They both instinctively looked back, and saw the kid flying down the stretch. Both John and Charlie sprinted with all that they had, encouraged by the added competition. The finish line was in sight, and all three runners sprinted with all that they had, and Charlie pulled ahead in the last twenty yards, pushing his body to keep going, winning the race, John placing second, and the kid from Iowa third. The crowd went crazy, and Charlie fell over with exhaustion, having just run the race of a lifetime. His strategy, which was simply a refusal to lose, worked.

"Great race," John said as he patted Charlie's back.

"Thanks, you too," Charlie barely got out, and was then helped into the shade by race attendants.

The bell rang for the second round, and like Charlie, Panther refused to lose. The fight plan, which was to win by decision, and work the body just didn't satisfy Panther. His ear was still ringing, and his focus became very direct, knock this man out. Ruthless stood four inches taller, and so he would have to lure him in lower, so as to get more head shots in. The two fighters came out like bulls, Ruthless striking first, a jab blocked by Panther. Another jab, and another. He was forcing him to keep his gloves up. Panther danced back, drew Ruthless in. Ruthless threw a reaching punch to the head, annoyed by the quick feet. His punch fell short by three inches as Panther leaned back like a swaying tower. Ruthless stumbled, and Panther pounced, quickly moving in, and delivering a powerful uppercut to the jaw. Ruthless's head flew back, then continued to fall forward, as Panther hopped to the side and delivered another shot to the head as Ruthless fell. The inmate crowd went crazy, and the referee started the count.

"One, two, three, four, five, six, seven, eight." And Ruthless pulled himself up onto the ropes, getting to his feet. He got the eight count warning, but he and his trainer kept on. The bell rang, and the fighter's cooled, and listened to their trainers.

"What's that all about?" Panther's trainer asked.

"I'm not going to let him beat me."

"He's not going to, but just stick to the game plan. You got 'im afraid, and tired, just keep moving, get low, pick up those body shots, and when he's off balance or off guard, take him out."

"Right." The bell rang for the third round, and Panther came out moving. He danced around the ring, barely letting Ruthless near, and when he did, he quickly avoided his shots, and returned body shots. It went on like this for most of the round, and then an exhausted Ruthless became overly frustrated and went in for a kill shot. Panther ducked, moved to the side, blasted shots to his ribs, then head, forcing him into the corner, opened his guard inviting a shot, exposing Ruthless's face, dodged his weak punch, and then WHAM! He delivered the bomb, knocking Ruthless out for the ten count. The referee raised Panther's arm in victory, and the crowd went crazy.

Four years passed after the epic race and the fight with Ruthless.

John was twenty-one, and a junior at the University of Illinois on an academic and athletic scholarship. Charlie, nineteen, also in college on a scholarship, was in his freshman year at the University of Kansas. They were both outstanding in the classroom, and in their athletic endeavors. Charlie quit running cross country, after he started to fill out with age, and began wrestling. His agility and strength took him to the state championships three years in a row, where he won twice in his junior and senior years. He wrestled for the University, as well as threw the shot put, and discus for the track team. John kept running, and was brought on to the University of Illinois' track team as a long jumper and sprinter. They were both exemplary students, as well. John was majoring in Biology, and Charlie, undecided still, was aiming at a degree in engineering. John had met a nice young woman, pretty as the day, and they had been going steady for a year.

"Do you wanna get some ice cream?" Sarah asked as she met John in the hall, outside of her English class. John met her with a little kiss on the cheek. She smiled and pushed her beautiful honey blonde hair over her shoulder.

"I wish I could, but it would go right to my butt!" John joked.

"Shut up!"

"You know I can't, but I'd love to watch you eat some," he said then quickly tapped her butt.

"You're bad!"

"You know it. The conference championships are going to be epic this year. I've gotta be as trim as possible, aero dynamics!" he said as they walked through the halls of the university, and over to the commons. "Ice cream here, or off campus?"

"Off campus," she said with a little smile.

"Alright, let's ride. Let me check my mailbox first though, o.k.?"

"O.k., me too."

John took his keys from his pocket, one for his dorm room, the other for his motorcycle, and the other his mail key. He pulled them out, already having fingered the right key, stuck it in the slot, turned the key to the right, and opened the door. A lone letter sat, and for some reason or another the letter caused him to pause. A vision of his father in the woods flashed into his mind, then quickly out. He could sense his spirit from the afterlife, but little did he know his father was alive, and thinking of him. He grabbed the letter and inspected the outside of it. Could his suspicion be true? Was his father looking for him? This was a recurring thought that he quickly dismissed when it came, as it was always too painful. The letter was very formal in nature, return address, Washington, D.C. Sarah walked over to his side as he slid his key into the crevice of the sealed portion of the envelope. He pulled out the letter and read it. His eyes quickly moved to the heart of the letter, and then he dropped his arm as he held the letter.

"What, what is it?" Sarah asked with great concern for the look on John's face.

"We're officially at war now; it's a draft letter. I leave in two weeks."

"What?"

"Here, look." Sarah took the letter, and read it as John became aware of the other young men around him, opening the same letter. The sense of fear was thick in the air, and it was even thicker on John's chest. "Oh my God, John, what are you going to do?"

"What do you mean? What am I going to do? I have to go."

"We could leave the country, go to Canada, Mexico. John, are you listening?" John had a look of intensity coupled by a weight of fear.

"Huh, I know, it's o.k. I'll be fine. We don't want to run."

"Aren't you scared?" Sarah asked as tears came to her eyes. John was lost in his thoughts, envisioning war.

"Yeah, I am," he said as his knees got weak.

3

MEANWHILE, OVER ON THE UNIVERSITY OF KANSAS CAMPUS, THE SUN was shining, and it was spring. The winter blues had been shook, and Charlie trotted through the campus, wondering why the mood wasn't as upbeat as usual. He saw one of his buddies, and jogged over to him, with books in hand.

"Chris, what's up?" he asked as his friend leaned against a tree.

"I'm going to war."

"Huh? Why?"

"There's a draft, check your mailbox, you'll probably be going too."

"What?"

"Yeah, man, I can't get quite get a grip on it myself."

"Man, I can't go to war, I've got a meet coming up," Charlie said shaking his head, not wanting to accept what Chris was saying. He took off for the commons, checked his mail, and there it was. The letter.

A week later Panther was released from prison on exemplary behavior. He had served eighteen long years of a twenty-five year sentence. He had finally made some progress, through his continued

54

letter writing, as to his children's whereabouts. He was told, however, that he would have to go in person to the individual county offices, and search the records himself. So, when he got out, that's what he did. He went, searched, and found. It turned out that both John and Charlie's last foster placements were the only ones on record, and so he sought the families out, in hopes of finding his children.

A couple more weeks passed, and as Panther attempted to contact the parents who adopted his children. His children were starting basic training at the Great Lakes Naval Boot Camp as they were both called into the navy. Panther dialed the Morrison's first, no answer, so he hung up the phone and dialed the Rosenthal's. Ring, ring, ring, ring, ring. Panther's heart was pounding.

"Hello?" a woman answered.

"Hello, Mrs. Rosenthal?"

"No sir, she ain't home right now, can I ask who's callin'?" the woman said in a kind way.

"Um, yes, I'm Lakota's father, I mean John, and I was just um, trying to . . . I was trying to find my son."

"Oh, I's not supposed to say sir, though I sure would like to."

"Right, that's what they told me over at social services, but if you can just hear me out. I'm a good man. My boys were torn away from me, by circumstances that I couldn't control."

"Oh, I see."

"I love my boys, ma'am, and if you could just give me a hint, I would appreciate it," Panther said as he choked on rising emotions.

"Oh, now, I sure wish I could sir, but . . . ."

"Please ma'am, my heart is hurting, and I need to find my boys."

"Well, I don't know about boys, but I know about John. Does he have a brother?"

"Yes, of course, he doesn't know that?"

"No, sir, and I'm not sure who did. And besides, John's a man now."

"Right, but he'll always be my little boy," Panther said as a tear came to his eye, and the Rosenthal's old maid could feel his heart.

"Oh, sir, I understand. I've a youngin' myself. Grown, but always little in my heart."

"So? Can you help me?"

"He's been called to war, sir."

"What?"

"Yes sir, he's been called into the Navy, straight from his junior year at the great University of Illinois, such a smart boy, athletic, handsome as can be."

"Oh my God, Lakota," Panther's heart sunk to his stomach, and the once welling tears fell onto his cheeks.

"Sir, he's at the Great Lakes Naval Boot Camp."

Panther could hear a voice in the background, and a door shutting.

"I've got to go," she whispered. "God bless you, sir," she said and hung up the phone. Panther fell back against the phone booth wall, and slid down to the ground. He cried as he tucked his head down into his legs.

"Hey! Come on!" an impatient, perturbed man said and banged the booth with his hand. Panther rose up, wiped his face, and the man instantly stepped back with a look of horror. Panther's eyes were now fierce and determined. He ripped open the phone booth door, pushed the man aside and headed straight for the bus station. He bought a one-way ticket to the Naval Station. He spent all the money he had earned in prison but a few dollars and then tried to call the Morrison residence one more time before he boarded the bus. He put the coins into the slot, and waited for someone to pick up on the other end.

"Hello," Mrs. Morrison said as she answered the phone.

"Um, yes, I'm a friend of Charlie's, from high school, is he home?"

"I'm afraid not, he's been called into the Navy. May I ask who's calling?"

"Oh . . . yeah, I was in his science class, we weren't really friends, but more like classmates."

"O.k., sorry to tell you, but he's in boot camp. You haven't been called?"

"Yes ma'am, I have," he said with his continued younger voice.

"Is that what the call's about?"

"Yes, I was just wondering where he was headed, so that I might contact him. This whole war thing came at a bad time, I wanted to tell him about a great opportunity, a discovery really, after this is all over that is," Panther made up the story as he went along.

"Oh, fantastic. Well, he's at the Great Lakes Naval Boot Camp, so . . ."

"O.k., thank you, ma'am, thank you so much."

"O.k., you be careful, and come back safe."

"Right, thank you." Panther hung up the phone, and his heart started to race with the knowledge of both of his boys being in the same place. They didn't know each other, nor that they were right there together. Nor did they know that their father was alive and coming for them. He was elated, and ready to enlist, ready to be with his children.

He boarded the bus, looked around at the faces on the bus, mainly white, and was ushered to the back with the other coloreds by the bus driver. As it is with human curiosity, especially on a bus, especially with the man of Panther's stature, physique, color, and race, the people stared. Panther kept his eyes forward, and made his way to the back. He found an empty seat next to an old black man, pushed his bag into the compartment above, and sat down. He sat with his hands clasped on his lap, and envisioned his task before him, as he had been doing for the last twenty years. He twiddled his powerful thumbs, and kept his eyes forward.

"Chicago huh?" the old man said.

"Uh, yes sir, thereabouts," he said with a slight smile as he turned his head to the man.

"Chicago's a great city."

"Oh yeah," Panther said with a little smile.

"Yep. I can't wait to see that giant lake. They say it's like an ocean."

"Yes, that's what I hear," Panther looked forward again, assuming the short conversation had ended for the time being.

"Oh yeah, it's a great lake, literally you know."

"Right."

"Yeah, I'm getting too old to live on my own now, so I'm moving in with my daughter and son-in-law."

"You, too old?" Panther said trying to be kind.

"Yes sir, eighty-two, and counting. If it were up to me, I'd stay right here, and just die in my chair. I lost my wife three years ago, and they've been trying to get me to move in since, but I've always been stubborn."

"Sure, I can understand that. A strong will's a good thing, just so long as you put it to good use."

"You know, I've never heard anyone put it like that before," the old man said with a smile, and Panther smiled back. "You've got family in Chicago?"

"Oh well, yes sir, I sure do."

"Kids?"

"Yes, sir."

"Oh well, please, call me Hops, all my friends do," the man said as he extended his hand to Panther.

"Oh well, sure. My name is Panther," he said and took his hand.

"Panther, huh?"

"Yeah, it's Lakota."

"Oh, right."

"Hops, huh?" Panther said with a smile.

"Well it ain't African," Hops said with a smile. "When I was a boy I broke my foot puttin' shoes on a horse, wasn't holdin' 'im right, and he stomped down on my toe. It busted in more places than I even knew, so, I walked on crutches for a few weeks, and then hopped for another couple of months while the thing healed. So, they all called me Hops."

"O.k., well nice to meet you, Hops," Panther said with a smile and then put his head back to rest. The old man looked out the window, as the bus motored along.

Panther dozed off for the next couple of hours, going in and out of consciousness, as his head fell forward and back. He woke to the old man snoring away with his head resting against the window. Panther noticed some other passengers looking at Hops in a not so favorable way, and so he gently woke the old man.

"Hops," he said as put his hand on his shoulder and shook it a little bit.

"Huh? I am, just a few more minutes," he said in a dream state.

"Hops, hey, you're snoring," Panther said smiling at the old man as he tried to wake him up.

"Huh, what?" Hops responded as he woke up in a startled manner.

He put up his fists while drool ran down his cheek. Panther couldn't help but laugh. And, he couldn't stop laughing. Something he hadn't done in quite some time. "What?" Hops responded seriously but then realized his fists were up. He joined Panther in laughing. It felt good to Panther's soul as they carried on.

The rest of the trip was mainly quiet, with a couple of stops on the way. The bus pulled into the station, Panther grabbed his bag, and said goodbye to his bus mate Hops.

"Alright Hops, it was nice to meet you, maybe we'll meet again," Panther said with a smile.

"Well, let's just hope I make it that long," Hops said with a smile, and Panther smiled back. "Hey, put your will to good use, huh," Hops said. "Never take no for an answer."

"Yes, sir, thank you, I'll see ya," Panther said and Hops tipped his hat. Panther made his way out of the bus station, and went straight to a recruiting station. He walked in tall and proud, ready to enlist. He knew that he was still of age, and confident that they would take him in. He wouldn't take no for an answer.

"Yes sir, may I help you?" the older man dressed in military garb sitting behind his desk asked, as Panther walked in.

"Yes, sir, I would like to enlist in the Navy."

"O.k., I see, well, have a seat, and we'll talk some things over."

"Sure, thank you," Panther said and sat down.

"I assume you are a U.S. citizen?"

"Yes, sir."

"May I see your I.D., please."

"Yes, sir," Panther said as he pulled his wallet from his pocket, and gave him his newly issued I.D.

"Oh, fresh out of prison, huh?"

"Well, yes sir, but it's not as it seems."

"And how's that?"

"Well, it was self-defense. I was forced into a situation."

"I see, well, let me get on the phone, and see what the deal is." The man picked up his phone and dialed the warden at the Colorado State Pen. He spoke to the warden for a few minutes, hung up the phone, and then continued to speak with Panther.

"So, I spoke to the warden, and he tells me you are quite a man."

"Well, I try to be."

"He says that not only are you a boxing champion, and a decent human being, but he also says that I would be a fool not to allow your enlistment. The only problem is you need special permission to enlist. We can't send convicted felons to war unless you're granted permission by higher ups."

"Oh, I see," Panther said and briefly hung his head.

"Yes, well. I'm afraid my hands are tied here, sir," the enlisting officer said as he sat back in his chair and folded his hands.

"If I might be honest with you, sir," Panther said as he readjusted himself in his chair.

"Yes, please be."

"My children, sir."

"Huh, I'm not following. Please clarify."

"Well you see, sir, did the warden tell you about my case?"

"Briefly, not in detail, only that you were an exemplary inmate, and that you got on well with everyone."

"Well, my wife was killed, right in front of my eyes. My children were to be next, I acted in defense of them, and well sir, I killed the man that killed my wife. I thought about running, but didn't want to endanger my children. I was a U.S. citizen, and I expected a fair trial, which I did receive. My children grew up without a mother, or a father, and now they are both enlisted in the navy. They were separated as babies, then grew up with different families. They don't even know each other, or that I'm even alive. I'm still young enough to serve, strong enough, and willing to do whatever it takes to be with my boys."

"So you have no interest in serving your country? We could arrange a visit, if that's all this is."

"No, sir, that's not all that this is. I am willing to die for this land, no matter who stakes claim to it, and I am willing to do it by my children's side. I will not live another day without them, and a visit will not do. I will be a great asset to our nation, and I will prove this."

"O.k., well, I'll tell you what, you seem like the kind of man we could use. And, it happens to be your lucky day. I used to be a 'higher up.' WW1. These stripes aren't just for show. I just need to make a phone call to a friend of mine to get clearance. Then, if you can pass some simple tests, right here, then I will send you on to boot camp."

"Yes, sir. Fantastic, sir. Thank you," Panther said with reserved enthusiasm.

"Just give me a minute, will you?" the officer asked as he picked up his phone.

"Of course. Thank you."

He proceeded to make a very brief phone call as Panther sat nervously waiting. He hung up the phone.

"O.k.", the officer said with a little smile. "Permission granted."

"That's it? I mean . . . wow! I have a question, if you don't mind me asking sir?" Panther asked with relief and curiosity in his voice.

"No, ask away."

"Did you choose this post? I mean, no offense, I'm just curious,"

Panther asked as politely and carefully as possible.

"Yes, I did. I'm too old and tired to do anything else. Plus, I only do this twice a week to give the young bucks a break and to get away from the wife," he said with a wink and a smile. Panther smiled back.

"So, shall we proceed?" the officer asked.

"Yes, sir. Thank you, sir. Oh, and one other thing," Panther asked rather quickly.

"Yes, what is it?"

"There is not an issue of all of us being at war together? Is there?" Panther asked in a straight forward manner.

"If there was, I wouldn't be considering you as a candidate. The truth is, even if there were something to stop you all fighting together, which at this time there is not, you are not technically family. They are adopted I assume. Correct?"

"Correct," Panther said with a ping to his heart.

"All of you have a different last name. So, no. No issue."

"O.k. Thank you, sir."

Panther passed the tests with ease, including an intensive physical, vaccinations, eye exam, strength test, and then a haircut, all two feet of it.

"Lookin' good!" the recruiter said.

"Thank you, sir," Panther said as he rubbed his shaved head. "You don't have record of what regiment my children are in, do you?"

"No, sir, I don't, but it won't be long before you locate them, and if you have any trouble, just speak to your commanding officer, tell them I gave allowance. Now, this isn't going to be some kind of family picnic, you know that, right? You'll be lucky to see them briefly, and then after that, who knows. Everyone is shipped different directions after boot camp, according to strengths observed. You are not guaranteed a single thing."

"Right, yes sir, I understand."

He signed some paperwork, then stayed the night at a local mo-
tel, paid by the government, and then took the first bus out to the
station. He was the only forty-year-old on the bus, let alone Native
American. He caught some looks, but the looks were different than
on the other bus. In this bus there were looks of fear in young men's
eyes, not concerned with the color of the men's skin around them,
nor their age, but rather searching for comfort, or some type of com-
panionship, as they were all headed to the same place, and then on to
war. He sat next to a young white man, half his age, and introduced
himself. They rode in silence to the naval station, and then got off
the bus.

"Alright little boys, it's time to become men!" A Military Training
Officer shouted as they filed off the bus. "Oh, an Indian, this is rich!
Might have to get this one a cane!" he laughed. Panther knew this
was all part of the breaking-down process, and didn't pay any mind
to it. A recruit laughed at the commander's musing, and was quickly
confronted. "Something funny, boy?"

"No, well yeah, that was funny," the kid said trying to rally support
to no avail.

"Get down and give me twenty, then we'll see who's laughing. If I
say laugh, then you laugh; if I say cry then you cry; if I say jump, you
say how high, sir? Now get on the ground you little panty waist, and
give me twenty!" The young man, only seventeen, dropped to the
ground and tried to do the push-ups, but was only able to do about
twelve. The trainer put his foot on his back, and then spoke to the
crowd now standing watching. "No one steps out of line, or you'll
get your ass shoved down to the ground! Now march!"

They were ushered into the gates of the Naval Station, led past marching troops, and pushed into the decontamination station to be stripped of all of their civilian life. This was nothing new to Panther, as he stood naked among fifty other men in the showers. They were washed of their old, and entered into the new. They were given navy clothes to put on, showed to their living quarters, and given their navy bags full of all that they would need in the many days to come. They were shown how the bags were to be packed and unpacked. From the rolled mattress, hammock, blankets, to the rolled clothes. They had to pack and unpack it a dozen times, until everyone one got it right.

"This is crazy," one of the young men mumbled.

"What did you say?" Officer McCally said, as he moved quickly over to the unfortunate to be heard young recruit.

"Nothing, sir," he responded.

"No, I heard something, and you're going to tell me what," he said emphatically as he stood over the young man.

"I said that I feel crazy," he said as he lifted his eyes from repacking his bag for the tenth time.

"You stand at attention when you speak to me boy! To your feet!" The young man got up from the floor and stood at attention. "Now, is that what you said, or are you lying? Maybe I'll ask your buddy here, is that what he said? Huh, Mr. Redskin?"

"Yes sir, that's what he said. He said that he felt crazy, sir," Panther said as he rose up and stood by the young man's side.

"Well alright then, we're getting somewhere then, because we're going to have a whole lot of crazy going on, and you'll thank me when this crazy saves your lives. I want you all to listen, and listen good. Your world, the one that you have known, is going to be turned upside down, and if we don't do these things over and over, you'll be feeling even more crazy when you're under enemy fire. If we don't work as a team, as a unit, with strict rules, there will be chaos, and that's when the real crazy will come. So, if you don't like what and how we do what we do, then, well, you'll be the first to die. Do you want to die? Do you want to be responsible for your neighbor's death? We're at war, boys, and if you can't grasp the notion, well . . . you soon will. Now pack!"

The young man went back to packing his bag, and looked over at Panther in such a way as to say thank you. Panther briefly acknowledged his thanks, and then went on repacking. After they all had the order of items, and proper technique of packing and unpacking they were instructed to shoulder their packs. They were then ushered out of their barracks and led on their first of many marches with their packs lifted high upon their shoulders.

"Five, ten deep, it's not that hard, unless of course you people are truly retarded, and by the looks of this one I'm not so sure. Now fall in line!" the officer yelled. "On my count, it's left, right, left, right, got it! Now march! Left-right, left-right, left-right! Come on, it's lookin' sloppy, I know you all can walk! Now repeat it, left-right, left-right, left-left, left--left, left-right-left, left--left, left-right-left!"

They marched for the next two hours in this manner with many ready to fall over from exhaustion, from the weight of the packs, and the weight of the situation. Panther cruised along, all the while scanning the base, searching for his children. Just when he'd see a brown face, it would be Hispanic, or light black, not the Native American face he was looking for. He was looking for his and Anna's features, anything that would maybe single his boys out. He knew their last names, and was certain that it would only be a matter of days before he would find them. They finished their march, then went back into the barracks where they were further instructed on rules and regulations of the base, and given a handbook for the Navy's regulations in general.

"We eat at eighteen hundred hours, shower, shave, take a crap, make your beds, and then Officer Rosenthal will be in to instruct you further. He'll take you morons into the mess hall for some chow."

Panther thought nothing of the name, until he remembered that Lakota's adoptive family were the Rosenthal's. He thought it had to be a coincidence, and shrugged it off. "How would he be an officer in only two short weeks anyhow?" Panther thought, as he headed to the showers. He showered up, made his bed, and sat down on it. He was on the bottom bunk, and his bunk mate was the young man whom he had just stood by.

"Name's Sam, yours?" the young man said after hopping off his bunk.

"My real name? Or my American name?"

"Real name, of course."

"Panther."

"Nice, now we're talkin'! So what'll they call you around here, other than dirt bag, and boot?"

"Wes."

"Alright Panther, between me and you, I'd rather call you the mighty Panther, so that'll be just be our thing."

"Alright, and in the mean time I'll come up with a name for you, other than Sam, dirt bag, or boot. Sound good?"

"Yeah, sounds good to me," Sam said with a smile for the man twice his age.

Just as they were through talking, Petty Officer Rosenthal walked in, and spoke to the group of men.

"Alright fellas, I've been granted the great honor of showing you all the way to dinner. Aren't you a lucky group of men," John said sarcastically, and with a tone much lighter than the Training Officer. They had chosen John, as well as quite a few other young men, mainly educated, athletic, and with plenty of charisma to do light duty training, such as informing new recruits on some basics. He was also given greater responsibility within his own group of men, after showing leadership qualities right off the bat.

The men slightly laughed, but weren't sure how to react, so most stood at attention.

"It's a long road ahead of us, men, and I'd rather die with a smile on my face."

The men smiled. "But don't think for a second that I won't whip any of your asses if you second guess me, or your commanding officers. Within two short weeks I've learned that this is no game, and as we speak, men are dying. So if you want to join them, feel free; otherwise, you'll listen up, and listen good. Understood?"

"Yes, sir!" the men were instantly behind John. Panther looked at the fine young man as he began to walk the row of bunks, and knew it was his son. Emotions began to rise as Panther fought back tears. John walked to the end of the bunks, where Panther stood, and then looked him right in the eyes.

"Good to see we have such dedicated Americans among us. God only knows, and what He knows is that if I were your age, I'd be set upon my rocking chair smoking a pipe, full of God only knows what." The men laughed, but then stopped immediately as John looked around seriously. "Are you fit enough old timer?" John eyed the man before him, and he could clearly see the strength.

"Yes, sir," Panther said as he looked into his son's eyes.

"Let's have a look see, just for fun. You think you can outdo me?"

"No, sir."

"Alright, let's have some fun, first one to fifty push-ups wins," John said with a wink to the other men.

"Well, I don't know."

"Come on, don't make me order it," he said as he got onto the ground.

"Yes, sir," Panther said and then got into push-up position. They both started, same pace, one for one. They stayed this way for the next thirty pushups, and that's when Panther started to pull ahead. The men had gathered around at this point, cheering each of them on. Panther was at forty, John at thirty-seven. Panther's strength was just building, and was about to fly through the next ten, but then slowed, on purpose. He knew his son's respect was on the line, and so, he faked fatigue. John caught up, and then finished his fifty as Panther strained on his forty seventh.

"Alright, that's it. You had me worried there for a minute!" John said as he stood up.

"Yeah, I ran out of gas."

"Well, you know what they say, slow and steady wins the race, unless of course you're like the kid who whipped my ass by sprinting!" he said with a little laugh, then quickly wiped the smile. "At attention! Line up for chow!"

Wes, as he was now known amongst his peers, fellow boots, filed into the cafeteria. He grabbed a tray, was served his meal and sat down with his bunkmates. The stirring in him to talk to his son, at least he thought it was him, was too much to handle. And so, without permission, or without knowing whether or not it was the right time, he stood, and walked over to where Officer Rosenthal sat.

"Excuse me, sir, I'm not sure if this is allowed, but if I could have a word with you in private?" Wes asked as he looked about the table of unfamiliar faces.

"Well," John looked to his superior officer, and was given a nod yes. "Sure." John rose from his chair, and walked with Wes to the corner of the mess hall. "So, what is it?"

"Well, sir, I don't know how to say this, but before it eats me alive I must. I believe that I am your father." Panther looked at the tall, handsome man standing in front of him and could see his child by simply looking into his eyes.

"Excuse me," John said and looked deeper into Wes's eyes, and then around to see if anyone was looking.

"I called your home, in Chicago, when I got out of prison. They told me that I could find you here. Lakota, you're my son." John's eyes instantly welled with tears as his mind flashed back to the wintry woods, staring up at his father and then quickly to the jail cell where the screaming of his father haunted him for all of his life.

"Dad?" he said as a tear fell from his eye, but was quickly wiped as if it was a scratch. "Why didn't you come for us?" he said firmly yet quietly.

"The man that killed your mother, well, I killed him. You and Dakota were too little to survive the winter, and I had no choice but to turn myself in."

"So I really do have a brother?" John asked in the most composed manner that he could.

"Yes, and he's somewhere here, on the base."

"Oh my God, so, you're telling me that you came all the way out here, joined the navy, just to find us?"

70

"Yes."

"Well, what's my brother's name?"

"Dakota . . . Charlie Morrison."

"Charlie Morrison? Are serious? He's in my company."

"Now wouldn't be a good time to hug you, so I won't, but I've wanted to hold you every last second of the last twenty years, and I'm so proud of the man that stands before me. I'm so sorry that it's had to be this way," Wes said as a tear fell, and he quickly wiped it away.

"O.k. dad, it's o.k., I'll have a talk with Charlie tonight. He's not going to believe this. He was just so little. He's not going to have any memories. But, um, yes, I can make sure of that," John said as a man walked by. Panther nodded, and walked back to his table.

The first day came to a close, and the bugler played taps as Panther lied in bed. He wondered about the conversation his boys were having, and as he began to doze off he was visited by Anna in his near dream state.

"Don't worry, my love, they will stand by you, and know that you are their father. I will go to them in spirit, and call upon our babies to know. You will fix their broken hearts, and I will always be with you all," she said as she appeared in an apparition by his bed side. Panther didn't know whether he was awake or not, but felt at peace. He fell asleep that night, only to be awakened by the bugler, and the rattling of a baton against the steel frames of the bunks. Everyone jumped to attention, and rushed into their morning duties, mainly making their beds, securing their items, as well as quickly preparing for the first real day of basic training.

"Alright, ladies, time to stop jerking around. Today you become men, except for you, old man, you become more of a man. Calisthenics gentlemen! Outside, now!" Officer McCally yelled and his voice echoed off the metal barrack walls. The men hustled out, and got into five lines of ten. They followed the commands of their officer, going through a rigorous series of push-ups, sit-ups, up-downs, jumping jacks, running in place, stretching, etc. They then went for a five mile run, all before breakfast. They ate, then went to their first day of classroom.

"Alright, listen up, and listen good. Not only do your lives depend on it, but the guy's life next to you, as well. Let's make no mistake, we are preparing you for war. Our country is at war; our world, gentlemen, is at war. Thousands of men are dying as we speak. As Americans, it is our duty to defend our freedom. We only have six short weeks to prepare you all for the greatest challenge of your lives, and if you keep your eyes and ears open, push yourselves to your limits and beyond, then you will make it out of this war alive. Each and every one of you will be in combat, in one way or another, and without honor, courage, and commitment you will be the first to fall. You will be the first to let your country down. So, listen up, your life depends on it," the officer instructed, as he stood in front of the men. The intensity and reality was thick.

4

THE COMMANDING OFFICER BEGAN HIS CRASH COURSE, PREPARING the men as quickly as possible for the road ahead of them. When class let out, the boots were fed, and then the conditioning escalated as they ran, marched, drilled, swam, and pushed themselves to their very limits. Panther was always at the head of the group, to the surprise of everyone. He was the strongest, fastest, smartest, and had the most endurance of all of the men in his training company. The day came to a close, and as Panther sat down for dinner that evening, John was preparing to bring Charlie and his father together for the first time in twenty years.

"Boot Wes, if I might have a word with you," John said after tapping on his father's shoulder.

"Yes, of course," Panther said and rose from the table. He followed his son out of the doors to the mess hall, and there he stood: his baby boy, Dakota. Panther wanted to cry at the sight of his son. John put his hand on the back of his father's back, and then spoke.

"Charlie Morrison," John said.

"Yes sir?" he answered in a way that showed concern for the situation, as if he had done something wrong.

"Charlie, I'm your brother, and this is our father." Charlie's knees buckled, and an odd smile that wasn't really a smile came across his face.

"What?"

"Tell him, dad," John said as he looked to his father to clarify and convince.

"It's true, Charlie, I held you in my arms. Your mom and I named you Dakota, and your brother Lakota, after our great nation of the Sioux."

"So where's my mom?" Charlie said.

"No one ever told you boys the truth, about what happened that day, and I guess I can't blame them. They told you boys that we were both dead, but the reality is, only your mom is."

"What, this is some kind of messed up joke, right? You're my dad? And you, my brother? I have absolutely no memory of you guys, at all. This is a joke, right?" he said with a crooked smile, and a cracking voice from the rising emotions.

"No, Charlie, it's not. I remember dad, and I remember the day he had to turn us over to the state. Tell him, dad."

"Well, I had come home from hunting, happy as could be. You guys were my everything and I couldn't wait to show you the deer I had gotten. When I walked in a man was in the process of killing your mother, and so I killed him. I tried to run with you boys, but it was the dead of winter, and you guys were just babies. They would have hunted us down, and killed us all. I had to turn myself in, and that's when they took me to prison. At the same time your mother's family was killed in a tragic fire, and all of my family was dead, too. There was no other option for you boys. It broke my heart, and there hasn't been a second that I haven't thought about you, and wanted to hold you," Panther said, as tears started to well, and his voice fluctuated from the powerful words.

"So you joined the navy to be with us?" Charlie asked.

"Yes, and I never want to leave your sides ever again," he said as tears began to pour out. John hugged his dad from the side, and Charlie stood motionless, stunned.

"So," John said with a little laugh after the tears. "We go to war together!"

"Yep, I guess so," Charlie said with confusion in his eyes.

"Just so long as I can keep up with you guys," Panther said with a smile for his boys as they headed back to the mess hall.

Boot camp flew by, and at the end of the six weeks the boots were now officially Navy men. There was a small ceremony, a day to visit with family, and then off to war. Except, in the course of basic training, forty men were chosen to go down to Florida for further training. These men showed exceptional strength, endurance, swimming abilities, marksmanship, and great leadership. Among these men were Wes, John, and Charlie. They were shipped down to Fort Pierce, Florida and then to the reefs off Hawaii to train as UDT (Underwater Demolition Team) a.k.a. frogmen, an elite core of Navy men.

"You forty men have been chosen because you are the best of the best, but not all of you will make it through the next couple of weeks. In the next twelve days, you will be tested like never before, and half of you will be sent packing, off to another duty. Twenty will remain. The fact is gentleman, we are in urgent need of men who can become supernatural, and as a result make way for our troops on to the islands. There are hundreds of yards of coral reef, inhibiting our ships to make land fall. We have lost thousands of men, having to stop short and wade in. We are being gunned down, without even a chance of getting onto the island. It will be your task to dive, place explosives on the reefs, detonate the devices, and then be the first on the islands. We will then pull in our ships, deploy our men, and take the island," the commanding officer said, as he paced back and forth in front of the group of forty men. "The training starts now," he said as he stood in front of the crystal clear water in southern Florida. "What we are asking of you men is like nothing we've ever asked any of our men, and it's going to require a great deal of courage. If you have any doubts in your mind about your ability to carry out these duties, stand forward now, and save me the time of weeding out the weak." The men, standing at serious attention in formation, looked to see if anyone would indeed step forward, and not a one did.

"Good. Well, it's about time you got used to living in trenches, so pair off, and dig your new home. Shovels are there, empty sand bags over there, helmets right here and live fire begins in four minutes. Go!" The commander yelled as each man grabbed the man next to him. They had been in live fire training before, and knew that this was no joke. They scrambled for helmets, shovels, and as per training started digging in. One man dug down into the sand with the three foot shovel, building the sand in front of him, as his partner bagged it into a wall. They dug for their lives. At three and a half minutes a majority of the trenches were dug well onto the beach, accounting for high tide in an arching formation, with the top of the arch facing the beach, and trees beyond where the fire was about to come. The commander came over the bull horn, announcing the fire, and then it came. All the men got as low as possible into their trenches, secured their helmets, and waited for the fire to come. And as promised, and warned, it came.

"Crazy little mess we got ourselves into, huh," John yelled to his partner, his brother, as he secured his helmet to his head, and kept low.

"Yeah, if this isn't heaven!" Charlie managed to get out, while he spit out some sand.

"Can we talk later, man, like when we're not under fire?" Charlie said.

"Right, duck now, talk later." They stayed under cover for the next ten minutes, and then the bullets stopped.

Panther couldn't help but wonder what he had gotten himself into, as he laid there in the trench dug by his new-found friend. He couldn't help but wonder what his boys were thinking at a time like this, and if they were anything like him they were scared. Scared not for the bullets flying right now, but the ones to come. Were they prepared to die? He had missed out on their entire development, and was feeling inadequacy like never before. What words could he say, what comfort could he offer, and the thought of trying to come up with words tied his stomach into knots.

A commanding officer came over a bull horn and shouted for them to surface, and they did. John hopped to his feet, reached his hand out to his brother and helped him up. He couldn't help but wonder what he was thinking, and once he saw the look in his eyes he knew. He was scared, just like John, and just like his estranged father. They climbed out of their trenches, then jogged over into formation.

"Alright men, it's time to begin the process. A process that's going to weed out the weak, and find the elite few that will be able to carry out specific tasks. These tasks will not only save our country, but ultimately the world. For the next two weeks you will eat, breathe, and sleep water and sand. Sleeping will not be a priority, there is simply no time for it. In the next couple of weeks we will be swimming, diving, exploding, fighting, shooting, and learning jungle survival. It's a crash course, boys; there's no time to waste. Only the strongest will be chosen, and the rest sent on. You see your trench there? The one you just dug? It will be your home for the next two weeks. We are going to simulate, and prepare you for hell. And hell starts now," the commander said. "First things first, and that's to take to the water. You all have been chosen because of your abilities in the water, as well as out. So, I need four groups of ten, now!"

They embarked on small dingies and paddled out. John's heart pounded as he anticipated the unknown, he looked to his left, his brother, and to the right, his father. Not one word was spoken as they took to the crystal clear waters and the sun beat down. The glare from the water was intense, and then the commanding officer began to speak to the men.

"We will be making way for our ships, blowing up coral reefs which are impediments at this time. We will dive, no gear, only a face mask and snorkel, secure the explosives, and then we detonate. This is what we are going to master, here and now. The rest will be explained as we go along. So, first thing's first. We start with mock explosives, and get used to diving. In one minute we'll be at our destination."

They continued to paddle, and then stopped upon command.

"We will work clockwise, starting with you, old man," he said with a hard smile for Wes.

"Yes, sir," he said and then looked down into the deep water.

"But first thing's first, everyone strip down to their underwear, and keep your boots on. We're getting in the water before we do anything." The commander took out his clipboard, and stopwatch.

"We're going to tread water for thirty minutes, as a warm up, and then we'll work on our breath."

"Sir, why the boots?" a young man asked.

"You'll need them once you get ashore, won't you?"

"Yes, sir," he said not having a clue what was in store for him.

"We slide into the water, like damn ninjas, no splashes. Go." The men slid into the water and the time began. As they began to tread water, some of the men started laughing, trying to keep their moods up.

"Shut it!" They were quickly reprimanded. The men went ten minutes fairly easy, and then it started to become increasingly difficult. John looked at Charlie, and was met with an empty face, but one that he read clearly. A face that hated this, and all that it was leading towards. Panther treaded closer to Charlie, just to be closer to him. His face turned even more vacant, and he purposefully treaded further away. John could see the pain behind the front, and he didn't blame him. Ever since he told him about his father, the smile turned to anger, and an emptiness that wasn't about to be filled by a man he barely knew.

"Five left," the commander said as some of the men started to sink into the water, then bob back up to float on their backs. "Treading, not floating! Only four more minutes!"

"Shark!" a man shouted as he turned his head and eyed the ten-foot monster circling below.

"Keep calm, they smell fear, swim closer to the boat, you're isolated," the commander said confidently to the scared young fellow.

"O.k., o.k.," he said as everyone became nervous.

"Were not on their menu, they're merely checking us out."

"Sir, I disagree," Charlie said.

"Shut it, three more minutes."

"There's another!" someone else said.

"Keep your cool, we're in their territory. They're simply curious."

"Oh, my God!" the original shark spotter yelled as he lurched out of the water a couple of feet. "He punched me! Permission to come aboard, sir!"

"Two minutes, keep your cool."

"With all due respect, easier said than done."

The next two minutes seemed like an eternity, and finally the men were called back onto the boat.

"Thank God," the young man said. "Was that a tiger?"

"Yes, very good. You know your sharks," the commander said sarcastically. "Alright, off with the boots, and on to the next exercise. Drink your water, and then we'll get started."

"Some first day," John said as he looked around with a smile.

"Having fun?" the commander said.

"Yes, I mean no . . . what I meant to say was, I'll keep my mouth shut."

"Good idea. Now we're going to get used to holding our breath, then dive to incrementally greater depths. We have flags below, each at different depths of the reef, and we will be having a little competition as to who can dive the deepest, as well as hold their breath the longest."

"Sounds like a great game," Charlie said.

"Oh yeah, well just for that smart ass remark you can go first. Into the water!"

He waited for Charlie to take a last drink, and then without looking at anyone Charlie slid into the water.

"Here's your first mine, take it to the first flag, and then come back up for the second. The trick is to take several fast breaths, and then a few large ones. You'll hold your last breath and then calmly, but quickly dive to the flag. Got it? Here's your mask. Now, you all listen, pause at about ten feet, grab hold of your nose and gently force air into your nasal and sinus cavity. Then, go from there." Charlie looked over at the other boats as they did the same. He did as he was told, and then dove into the water. He swam down, focusing solely on the flag, and his task. The pressure started to build, even at ten feet, he blew out some pressure and then descended another ten to the flag. He placed the weighted mine, and darted for the surface. He couldn't believe how difficult it was to dive only twenty feet, and was gasping for air when he surfaced. He played it cool though, and said no problem. "Gimme the next one," he said confidently. This one was set at thirty feet.

"You're alright?" the commander asked.

"Sure."

"Ears blown?"

"No, I'm good," he said shaking his head.

"Listen, on this next one, I want you to pause at ten, blow, then go twenty, blow, and then if you can, go thirty. If not, high tail it back up. Got it?"

"Yeah, I mean, yes sir, no problem."

Charlie took ten deep but quick breaths, then a huge breath before turning his head down and kicking his feet with great power as he dove. His brother and father looked at him descending, then looked at each other.

"He's got some balls," John said to his dad.

"Yeah. . . ." Panther watched as his son kept going deeper into the water. "He sure does."

81

"Hey, don't worry, he'll come around. At least I have memories of you, ya know," John said as he looked into the water with his father.

Charlie resurfaced, and his dad was right there to meet him, extending his hand to help him onto the boat.

"It's alright," he said out of breath. "I got it, I'm good here," he said as he held onto the side of the dingy.

"Alright, who wants to go deeper?" the commander said, as he looked around the boat.

"I do," Charlie said. "I'm just getting used to it, let me go another ten, and then I'll take a break. "

"Alright, if you insist."

"I do sir, respectfully."

"Alright, forty feet, place your weight, and then calmly, but quickly get your ass back up to the surface."

"Yes, sir." He took his breaths and went for forty. He made it to thirty, equalized pressure, and felt like his head was going to implode. His pride wouldn't allow him to stop. He kicked harder, thirty-eight, then a surge of energy, forty. He placed the weight onto the ledge of the coral reef, and then turned for the surface. He slowly blew out bubbles as he kicked his legs and surfaced. He broke the surface, gasped for air, and then with a light-headed hyperness declared he was done. The men helped him up onto the boat, and it was at this point that he instantly gained everyone's respect.

"Nice work," one of the men said.

"Thanks," Charlie said as he sat and sipped on water from a canteen.

"Alright, I'll go next," John said.

"Alright soldier, you know the drill. You saw what and how, so get to it. Start at ten."

"Any advice, Charlie?" John asked his brother as he prepared to slide into the water.

"No, not really. Just sprint, it's how I've done everything," Charlie said.

"O.k." John said and then prepared to dive. Just as he was about to go under, he overheard Charlie talking on the dingy.

"I once ran in a cross country race, a huge meet, regionals, I was the youngest kid, and I had no plan other than to sprint the whole way," Charlie said to one of the guys on board.

"So, what happened?" the guy asked.

"I won," he said and then smiled. John flashed back to the kid who ran his heart out, and he couldn't help but think if it was his little brother. A sense of pride, and nostalgia came over him, coupled by a newly lit fire under his ass. He dove to ten, came up. Dove to twenty, came up. Dove to thirty, surfaced. Dove to forty, feeling like he was going to die, surfaced and then insisted he could do fifty.

"Are you sure soldier?" the commander said.

"Yes, sir," John replied looking extremely fatigued.

"Hey, don't do it just to beat me, John. I mean, c'mon man," Charlie said.

"Yeah, he's right John, maybe that's enough," Panther said with concern,` as he leaned over the boat.

"No, I got this," John said, took his breaths, went to fifty, placed the weight, and surfaced. He was helped aboard, and sat down next to his brother. Charlie handed him a canteen.

"That's pretty deep, huh? Don't worry, I'll be doing sixty, tomorrow," Charlie said with a smile for his brother.

"That was you, wasn't it?" John said out of breath.

"Huh, what are you talking about?"

"The race, regionals. You were the kid from Kansas. I was in that race. I came in second."

"What? Shut up . . . you were?"

"Illinois, the favorite to win."

"Oh man, that's wild," he said with a smile. "Sorry about that. I just kept running, and I wouldn't allow myself to stop, or let anyone pass."

"Yeah, I know the feeling."

"Well, hey, at least we both got our asses whipped at nationals. That kid from California, born in Africa, he ran like nothing I had ever seen. Beautiful," Charlie said and smiled.

"Yeah, he was something alright," John said and then took a drink from the canteen.

"Alright, I'll go next captain, sir," Panther said.

"Alright, go for it. Remember the deal."

"Right," he said and slid into the water. "Am I placing more weights, or do you want me to retrieve?"

"Easy there, old man. We can just reach down and grab the ten-foot weight!" the captain said, and the men started to laugh.

"Right, good one. So, should I retrieve the weights or what, sir?"

"Yeah, do that, good luck."

Panther took his breaths, momentarily closed his eyes, clearly focusing, and then dove. He quickly surfaced with the two weights from ten, then brought up the two from twenty, then the two from thirty, then the two from forty, and then the one from fifty. The men watched in amazement as Panther systematically, and seamlessly surfaced then dove once again. He grabbed one of the weights, and then went for sixty.

"He's got some stamina, huh?" John said as he looked over into the water and then back to his uninterested brother.

"Yep," Charlie said with an unimpressed look on his face.

"Man, you just don't get it do you," John moved in closer to Charlie to speak more privately. "Just because you can't remember him, that doesn't mean your time with him doesn't exist. He used to rock you to sleep, feed you bottles, tickle you, and loved us so much. Why else would he be here now?"

"I don't know, man. I'm just dealing with some stuff, so back off."

"Hey, you two. Cut the crap."

"Yes, sir," they said in unison. It was then that Panther surfaced with the weight in hand.

"I was just about there," he said out of breath. "I just couldn't make the last few feet."

"Well, old man, that was pretty impressive," the captain said.

Night fell on their trenches, and the men settled in.

"It's not the Ritz, but I guess it'll have to do," John said as he leaned back against the trench wall and looked out over the moonlit ocean. He watched the waves sally and suck back on shore, and listened to the constant drone of the breaking waves.

"Why, you've been to the Ritz?" Charlie wondered, then lit a cigarette.

"No, but I hear it's nice. Those things will kill you, ya know."

"Yep, that's the point. Who wants to live until their crapping themselves, not remembering their own name in some nursing home? I figure I'll get a head start on the rest of you fools."

"Nice theory, so how do you plan on holding your breath for even longer with all that tar in your lungs."

"Easy, I just do it. Give it a rest will ya, it's not like you're all of the sudden my older brother giving me advice. I'll tolerate ya, and maybe even be willing to learn more about ya, but just don't push it. You, or the old man. How is it that you can be all, I don't know, chummy with our father after years of nothing? Aren't you a little bit pissed? I don't know about you, but I went through some awful . . . .," Charlie paused and looked down. "And I'm not sure if I can just be all hunky dory about everything. I mean, didn't we have any other family? Why were we just shoved off?"

"I do have anger, and I went through just as much as you did, believe me. Apparently dad's family was all dead, and mom's family too. Her mother and father's home was burnt down. They were all killed in the fire."

"Oh, well . . . . how do you know all of these things?"

"I did some research. And I knew dad was alive too, in prison. My foster parents told me he was dead, but I didn't believe it. Not our dad, no way."

"Yeah well, I don't know. He should've busted out, and came for us."

"He probably tried, or thought about it anyways. But then what? Kidnap us? Be on the run with a convict, having the police hunt us all down?"

"Yeah, I would've taken that any old day over the nightmare I was in."

"Yeah, well, I don't know what to say. He loves us, and if you don't see that, then you're just blind."

"I'm not blind. I'm just messed up."

"I understand."

"So how's about we just try and get some sleep, huh?"

"Sounds good, goodnight," John said and then tipped his helmet down over his eyes, crossed his arms and shut his eyes. Charlie stared off into the water, thinking of the war to come, and the restlessness in his soul. Sleeping sounded good, but the agitation wouldn't allow it. He looked at the moon, so far away, and envied its position. He shut his eyes, and eventually nodded off to sleep.

Not too long after they fell asleep, John was rudely awakened at gun point.

"You both can't sleep at the same time! Now look at the mess you're in," a senior officer said as he smiled at John. John looked around in a daze, saw Charlie fast asleep, and then looked to the other trenches where the same thing was happening, men at gun point. "One of you's gotta stay watch, right?"

"Yes, sir, right sir," John said as he sat up straight and righted his helmet. "Wake your partner there, and get into formation."

"Yes, sir." John stirred Charlie, and they went over into the formation.

"One man has to stay watch gentlemen. Shoot, that's basic, isn't it? True, there is no enemy, but we will treat every minute as if there is. Understood?"

"Yes, sir!" they all said in unison.

"So, it's time for a little swim. Tonight's objective is to dive, place, and detonate an underwater mine. It's time for the real thing boys, there's no time to waste. We will be in the same groups as before. We're taking the dingies a half mile out, at which point we will dive and detonate. Then, we will swim the distance to shore, dig new trenches, and be ready for live fire."

Everyone's hearts started to beat heavily with the anticipation and nervousness of the training mission. They loaded into the boats, and set off. When they were a half mile out, they were debriefed, and a seasoned diver went down, placed the mine, swam back to the boat, then they waited. BLAM! The water shot fifty feet into the air, and the jaws of the men dropped at the site.

"God Bless America!" one of the men shouted.

"Zip it soldier. Now, we swim. In the water. Masks on. To the beach."

The men slid into the water.

"What about sharks?" one of the men asked.

"They can't see you. Just don't swim like a retard."

"What about the moonlight?" the man asked.

"Well then it will be a romantic dinner for Mr. Sharky. Now shut up and swim."

The men began to swim, and did so until they reached the beach. They bunkered down in the trenches, and stayed low. Within minutes, live fire came, then ceased after about ten minutes. The men took turns sleeping, and then morning came.

"Some night, huh bro?" John said as he rubbed his eyes, and picked out some eye crust.

"Yeah, some night. Wonder what's next."

"Food I hope, maybe some coffee . . . ." John said as he looked around. Just as he was, the commanding officer came over the megaphone and announced that rations would be delivered to their trenches, and not to move from their positions. So, they waited.

"Man, I've got to crap," Charlie said with a look of desperation.

"Go for it."

"You heard him, we can't move."

"That didn't stop me from crapping last night while you slept. I just dug a little hole next to the trench, and bombs away. I buried it like a cat."

"Alright, that's verging on too much information, but, alright. Don't you look my way; otherwise, I won't be able to go."

"Right, like I want to watch you."

"What did you wipe with, man? There's nothing here to wipe with, huh . . . what did you use?"

"I ripped off part of my t-shirt, worked like a charm . . . buried it too."

"Alright, look the other way . . . which side did you use? I don't want to dig up your turd."

"That side."

"The side I was sleeping on? You're just short of a dozen aren't you? Thanks."

"Well, I didn't want to be seen! Sorry!" John said trying not to laugh.

"Alright, well I'm going to your side, so I don't dig your same hole. Cover me." Charlie proceeded with his business, and just as he was wiping with a ripped part of his own t-shirt, a training officer walked over and gave them their rations for the next five days.

"Have a good one, Charlie? Hope it all came out well!" the officer said. Charlie quickly pulled up his pants, and kicked sand over the business. "Oh, yeah, there's some toilet paper in this sack."

"Great timing, really great timing," Charlie said sarcastically as he looked to both of the men, now laughing. "Yeah, real funny. Keep on . . . I'll get my kicks from one of you sooner or later, probably sooner."

"Alright, alright. Everything that you guys are going to need for the next little while is in this sack."

"Morphine?" Charlie asked.

"No, that's for later. When you get shot."

"Right, can't wait."

"Alright fellas, you got a half hour, do what you gotta do, and then fall in for instruction."

"Yes, sir," they both said in unison.

The men all stood in formation, at attention.

"Alright, hand-to-hand combat, gentlemen. That's the focus for the morning. You will be first on the island, and you must be prepared to fight in close proximity. This will also serve you when you want to go undetected. You'll be able to dispense the enemy, quickly and efficiently. So, we will demonstrate the first technique, then you will partner up, and go through the motions. I know a lot of this will be review but we are focused on staying sharp and learn new things, as well."

The commander and an officer went through the first three hand-to-hand combat techniques, ones they hadn't seen before, and the men watched.

"If we can't stab, then we fight with our hands, feet, teeth, elbows, knees, and heads. There is no love in war, gentlemen. It is either you or them, and we are going to make sure that it's not you. There is no such thing as "dirty" fighting in war; it's all dirty. This will be brief, and then on to our specific tasks in the water."

Their training flew by in a haze of endless water, sand, survival, detonations, and live fire. At the end of the week, twenty-two men were sent to Hawaii for another six days of specific mission training/debriefing, and the rest were assigned to applicable positions. John, Charlie, and their father Wes boarded a naval plane among the top twenty-two, destined for Hawaii. They stood near the landing strip, naval sacs in hand, waiting for their plane to be fueled.

"So, here we go, dad, just like you wanted . . . off to battle. You couldn't have planned it any better," Charlie said to his father, as they stood with the rising sun shining in their faces.

"How else should I have done it?" Panther responded, as he covered his eyes from the glare of the sun.

"I'm not sure . . . I try not to think about it. At least we'll get to die together, who needs the whole living together, playing ball, cookout mess?"

"What are we talking about?" John said as he walked over.

"Nothing, nothing at all," Charlie said.

"No, we were talking about something, we were talking about life . . . and the life your brother wished he had. And you know, Charlie, I wanted that too, more than you know. But you will never forgive me, and I can't make you either."

"Oh, o.k., well, I don't know what to say," John said, and truly didn't know how to fix what was broken. But he thought that if he could share in Charlie's pain, it would maybe help. They all stood watching the plane being fueled, and John began to speak. "I remember coming home from trapping . . . I did that to save up some money . . . and my foster parent was in a particularly foul mood. Well, I always hid what I was doing. They had no idea, up until the point when word got out that I was selling mink furs. My foster dad found out, and well . . . after a day of heavy drinking . . . he wanted to make sure that I knew he was on to me," John spoke as they all looked at the plane, with the sun now positioned right above it. They both looked over to John when he continued to speak. "He took me out into the living room, called in his family to watch, tore my pants down and then beat me with a wooden paddle, then put his cigarette out on my back. He didn't stop until his wife pulled him away from me."

"I'm so sorry, John . . . I would have killed that man . . . I'm so sorry."

"Yeah, sounds like my life," Charlie said without emotion, and started to move towards the now fueled plane.

"Hey, hold on, I'm just trying to say that I know what you're going through, Charlie." Charlie stopped and turned around.

"Oh, is that right? My all-of-a-sudden-brother. We all had separate lives, and now we're supposed to be some happy family? Screw that, screw you, and screw you too Wes," he said and then turned away.

"What?!" John said not believing what he was hearing.

"No, no, hang on John. He's right. I shouldn't have expected anything else. I failed you boys. His pain is real, and so is yours."

"Yeah, well so is yours, dad. You failed us? How? By doing the right thing? I would have done the same thing."

"Just give him time. And if he chooses to find healing with me, and you, then he will. Otherwise, we can't control what he does, or how he feels."

"I guess, but I wish he'd cut you a little slack."

"That's not up to you or me."

The men boarded the plane for Hawaii. The soldiers were silent, thinking of what was to come, and the lives they would be leaving behind. Some stared at photos and read letters that they had just received before departing. John sat in his seat, separate of his family and read a letter from Sarah.

> *Dear Johnny,*
>
> *I can't believe this time has come, and I can't imagine what you are going through. The papers, and the radio are entirely consumed with this island campaign. I'm not going to lie, I'm so scared John. It just seemed like yesterday when we were happy in love, without a care in the world. I miss holding you, John. I miss the way that you look at me, and I just wish this whole nightmare was over. But hear me, John, and hear me loud. Because as much*

as I miss you, do not let that distract you. O.k.? You come home to me, John, and do whatever it takes to do so. Don't let my emotions slow you down, let them fire your soul. I need you to come home to me, John. I love you with all of my heart, and you, the father of my future children need to fight with passion, for me and your country. Come home to me, John. I'll be waiting.

With All of My Love,
Sarah

John fought back some tears, as he looked at the picture she sent of the two of them together. He was fighting the homesick, and then her words resonated in him. Use our love as fuel, and come back to me. This alone became his mantra. He took the picture, put it back into the envelope, and tucked it safely inside of his jacket pocket.

Panther looked out the window, knowing the impending hell to come. He couldn't help but flash back to the days where he felt most alive. The days when his family was one, and his little boys were happy and knew his love. When his childhood dreams were a reality. When his youth passion was in full color, when Anna's smile, and the warmth of his children made his life rich. He longed to heal the pain of the brokenness, and wished it wasn't at a time when they were about to face down the barrel of a gun.

Charlie slept. And while he slept he dreamt. And in his dream his mother came to him, a mother he didn't even have memories of.

"Charlie, my baby," she said in his dream as she hovered above him in apparition form as he stood motionless as an eleven-year old boy. "I'm sorry that they took me away from you, baby. My heart longs to return to your side and hold you again."

"Who's going to take care of me?" Charlie said in his dream.

"I will protect you, and your father is coming," she said and then started to fade away.

"Mom! Don't leave me, don't leave me!" Charlie screamed in his dream and in conscious reality throughout the plane.

"Charlie, Charlie," the soldier next to him said as he nudged him awake.

"Huh, what?" Charlie said as he looked around and then up into air. "I saw her," he said as he looked around again.

"Saw who?" the soldier asked.

"My mother."

Panther's heart sank to the floor as he heard his son calling out to his mother. He as well as everyone else that was awake clearly heard Charlie scream in desperation. They looked in concern, all feeling the emotions of their friend as their own were peaked.

"Poor guy," the soldier sitting next to Panther said.

"Yeah," Panther said as he clasped his hands, hung his head then leaned against the window, looking out into the clouds, looking for an answer.

5

THE MEN LANDED IN HAWAII, GIVEN THEIR VERY TEMPORARY LIVING quarters and were immediately debriefed by their commanding officer.

"We are landing on the island of Guam," the commander spoke confidently to the seated navy frogmen. "As you know, the Japanese are trying to secure these islands in order to set up bases closer to our western shore. It is our sole mission to prevent this from happening. Our main objective is to secure the islands, cut off supply to their troops attempting to stronghold these locations, and we will do it by an air, land, and sea. We are going to choke the life out of these men, before they establish on these islands. It is your duty to dive by the cover of night, return with their stronghold position information, and then you will dive to blast the reef after debriefing us on their gun sights, and lay of the land. You all know the drill, and you all have been chosen because you are the best of the best. So, in the next few days we will go through the motions, and warm up for the big game. That is all, dismissed."

The men headed to their barracks.

"Hey, what if they find out you two are brothers, and that's your dad?" Ricky asked Charlie as they walked off. Rick had taken to Charlie, and he to Ricky from day one of UDT training. "Didn't you know that there has to be one surviving male, meaning not every male from a family can go to war?"

"Huh? Man, you act like it's been a secret . . . you're just thinking of this now? Like they give a crap anyway, some orphan mutts; they could care less."

"Well, don't you care?" Rick asked.

"Not really. I could fight it, but why? Plus, that's not even a viable argument with the government. In my mind I'm not related to them. Plus, I'm in too deep now. Obviously. Look at us man. I want to kill some Japs anyways, man. Screw it, I'm not afraid to die. I have no name."

"Alright, Charlie, I got ya, man."

The men returned to the barracks, and got their things in order before chow. Panther followed behind Charlie, wanting so badly to grab a hold of him and tell him how much he loved him. But it wasn't the time, and so he decided to not do anything. He did, however, decide to show him something that he had been carrying around his neck since the day his father died.

"Hey, Charlie," Panther said just as his son was about to walk into their barracks.

"Huh," Charlie said, knowing that it was his father's voice, but wanted to keep going.

"Dakota, come here," Panther said as he stopped and waited for his son to turn around. Charlie didn't stop, and kept walking towards the door.

"Dakota!" Panther said louder, and more firmly. Charlie didn't stop, so Panther sped forward and grabbed his arm. Charlie quickly turned around, throwing his arm out from his father's grip.

"I'm NOT Dakota, old man!" Charlie said with anger and then pushed his father to the ground. A small crowd congregated at this point, wondering what was going to transpire. Panther looked up from the ground, making eye contact with his son, and he could see the intense pain that was within his soul.

"O.k., o.k. I just wanted to show you something . . . I'm sorry."

"Well. . . ." Dakota said with a shaking voice and welling tears in his eyes.

"I'll show it to you another time," he said as John came to his father's side and helped him up.

"There might not be another time, dad . . . what the hell, Charlie?" John said and then moved quickly into Charlie's face. "What's your problem?"

"Screw you, John, I could care less. I'm ready to die . . . I'm already dead."

John and Panther didn't know the depth of Charlie's pain. John had seen and been through hell, but Charlie had additional hell that was nearly impossible to heal.

"Give him a break," John said with angry eyes for his little brother.

"Whatever," Charlie said as an unstoppable tear fell down his cheek, and he quickly went into the barracks then straight to the bathroom.

"Move along fellas; there's nothing more to see here," John said as he wiped the dirt off his father's back. "Sorry, dad."

"Why is it that you don't have the same anger for me," Panther asked as the crowd dispersed and went inside.

"I do."

"Why aren't you showing it?"

"Because I love you, dad. I don't blame you for what happened.

Charlie, Dakota, must be going through something even more intense. I know what I went through . . . hell. But maybe it was even harder for him, I don't know. Plus I remember you. There's no way he has one single memory of you."

"I don't know what to say . . . or do. It was a white man who killed your mother, and now I am paying for his sins. I'm even about to fight in a war for a stolen nation. I have lost my children, and I have lost my respect, from my boys, and for myself. I was crazy to think that me coming for you boys would solve the problem, and heal the broken years. I can only imagine the pain you two went through. I am so sorry, Lakota. I have failed you both," Panther said as he fought the welling tears.

"You haven't failed me, dad, and listen, you need to rid yourself of this guilt. It's going to weaken you, and then we'll lose you for good. We're going to war . . . there's no avoiding that. You need to be strong, and if things are meant to smooth out . . . well . . . then . . . they will. Now's the time to focus."

"You're right, Lakota. You're absolutely right. I just want you two to know how much I love you, and loved you both. The future is uncertain, and before we face down the barrels, I wanted to bring that message. A message that comes from not only me, but your mother who comes to me. She stands by your side, Lakota, she stands by Dakota's side, and she stands by mine, along with your grandfather Eagle's Claw. They will protect us, Lakota," Panther said as he looked his son deep in his eyes.

"O.k. dad, o.k.," John said and then was abruptly interrupted by a rush of men headed to the mess hall, including Charlie. He walked right by.

The morning came for the Underwater Demolition Team to board their battleship. The men boarded, settled in for the six-day journey and the next thing they knew they were a day away. Hell awaited them. Each and every man was well aware of this fact. It was lights out early that night, and John sat propped up in his bunk staring at Sarah with the little light available.

"You really love her, huh?" one of the men, Will, said from his lower bunk, looking up at John in his top bunk.

"Huh, yeah man. She's the best."

"Got a beautiful figure or what?" Will said.

"Hey, watch it man, but . . . yeah, she does," John said with a smile as he looked down.

"So you guys are gonna get married when you get back, huh?"

"I don't know. I'd be up for it."

"What about her?"

"What, you think she'd turn me down?"

"No, I didn't say that. I'm just saying."

"Saying what?"

"Well you know how girls are; they always need a man around. Who knows how long we'll be gone. What if she finds someone else?"

"What? What did you say?" John said with anger in his voice.

"Take it easy man, I . . ."

"Hey you two shut up, tryin' to sleep here," a soldier said a few bunks away.

"Ah pipe down," Will said. "I was just saying, man, I'm not saying anything, I'm sorry, man. I've just had an experience before, that's all."

"Whatever. . . ." John blew it off, but was interested in his story. "Alright, so . . . what happened?" John turned his way, and put his head on his propped elbow.

"Well, I was dating this girl in college. Man, I was nuts over her. I thought I loved her . . . alright, I loved her. Well, anyways, I got the opportunity to spend a semester in a Canadian fishery, anyways, that's not the point. I was gone for about four months. We talked every week, and she told me how much she loved me. Ha! She was doing some guy, and stringing me along. How's that for a load of horse crap."

"Well, not Sarah, never, no way."

"Alright, I'm just saying, man, things change."

"Yeah well, damn Will, thanks for the encouraging words."

"I'm sorry, man, really, I'm sorry. I should've never said anything. I'm just bitter."

"No, it's o.k. I just trust her. You'll find someone else, someone you can trust."

"Yeah, well I hope you're right, and I hope that I live to see the day."

"I hope that I live to see my baby," another man said, who couldn't help but overhear their conversation.

"You will Kyle, we're makin' it through this, man," Will reassured him.

"How far along is your girl?" John asked.

"Four months . . . I'm scared. I don't know what I'm more afraid of . . . fighting Japs, or being a dad," he said with a smile that turned into wide eyes as his eyebrows lifted with seriousness.

"We're gonna be o.k. We'll just get in there, kick some ass, and get out. They won't know what hit 'em," John said confidently as he laid his head back on his pillow.

Right before John drifted off to sleep, he was quietly stirred by his commander.

"Huh, what, yes . . . sir?" John said as he turned from lying on his side and faced the voice.

"John, c'mon, we're having a little pow wow, hop to it."

John's heart started to race, got up and followed after. He looked around and about seven other men were following, as well. They met up in a debriefing room. John looked around at the company he was in, all in their shorts, and looked at the faces in the room. Among the faces were Charlie and his dad.

"Alright fellas, look around you, if you already haven't. This will be the first team in. Another team will be blasting, after you all return from reconnaissance. We're only a hop and a skip away. You have been chosen because you are the best of the best. You will be swimming by night, get the info we need, and get your asses back. That's it. First in command of this team is Wes. We need blast info, gun sights, enemy defense points and safe landing zones. As you know, this is not a cake walk. They will be waiting for you, so now is the time to be ghosts, at your best. In and out, alright. We arrive in one hour, get prepared. That is all."

They had already analyzed the island on aerial maps, the positioning of the reefs, and were prepared to do the task blindfolded. What they didn't know was the details, the ones the aerials left out, and that's where they came in.

"Sir, if I might ask a question?" Charlie raised his hand.

"O.k., go ahead Charlie."

"Would it be o.k. if I made a necklace out of a pair of Japanese testicles?"

"It's not the time to mess around, Charlie."

"I was just trying to lighten the mood, that's all."

"Yeah, well, o.k., yeah, bring back a sack of nuts." Everyone hesitantly laughed, but the mood didn't change. Then John spoke.

"Sir, if Charlie isn't prepared for this mission, then maybe he should stay back," John said and then looked over at Charlie.

"Screw you, John!" Charlie reacted.

"I'm just concerned. That's all," John said as he looked forward.

"Charlie, are you prepared for this mission?" the commander asked as he moved closer to Charlie.

"I just said I wanted to bring you some nuts. Is that not prepared?"

"No, it's not. I need focus, and no jerking around. So, I'm going to ask you again, are you prepared for this mission?"

"Yes sir, yes sir I am. I am prepared," Charlie said seriously, and then looked to John with a look of focus and understanding. A new mood took over the room. Intense focus.

"There's no time for fear, men. Now's the time to do your jobs, and do them well."

The men went back to their bunks, and prepared for war. John walked with confidence, and a fast beating heart. He secured his survival knife to his leg, along with a waterproof pad and pen into his shorts. He strapped his compass to his wrist, and grabbed his flippers and mask. It was a "naked warrior" mission, and so they were just in their shorts.

"Ready for this?" Panther said as he walked up to his son.

"Yeah, ready," he said with a look of intensity and focus that reassured his father.

"O.k., good. And Charlie?" Panther asked as he looked into the eyes of his son.

"I don't know. He'll do alright."

"O.k."

The group of eight men, so as to not be seen by the enemy, even though they were under the cover of night, gathered around the torpedo bay.

"Alright, this is what you've been training for, men, so do your jobs, and do them well. In and out, simple as that. No screwin' around, and I will see you back shortly," the lieutenant said as he looked at the men with confidence. And, one by one, they were shot out of the torpedo tube. They swam under water until it was necessary to take a breath, and then slowly surfaced, only to return to swimming underwater. They were like silent seals in the night, undetected, and each focused on the task at hand.

They all made it to the shore, swimming right over the coral without a snag. They made land fall, crawled into the bushes, and then got busy with their task at hand. They each had a duty, and started towards the completion of these tasks. One man took a sand sample, another sketched the beach line by the light of the moon, and another still sighted potential impediments to their landing. Others attempted to spot gun sights, and strongholds. They all went about their business with stealth, like panthers in the night. Panther was no exception. He motioned with his hands for his men to stay put as he silently crawled further to get a better look at a potential gun sight. John nodded in agreement as he grasped his knife tightly in his sweaty hand. He watched as his father disappeared into the bush. Everyone crawled back, each done with their task. It was then that they were informed by John that Wes had crawled in, and they were to remain put until he returned. It was then that the worse-case scenario happened. John felt that his father had been gone too long, only a few minutes, and so he crawled into the bush as well. He came to where the bush about opened, and it was there that he saw his father being dragged silently with a knife held to his throat by two Japanese soldiers. John's heart started to pound, his mind raced, and just as he was about to rush the men, Charlie came up behind him. John made room for Charlie to crawl and see. Just as Charlie did, Charlie nodded no, and quickly crawled backwards, pulling on John's leg as he went. He dragged his brother back, and they both crawled out quickly.

"No John, we have a mission. These men need to go now!" Charlie said emphatically with a whisper.

"Right." John looked at the horrified and confused men. "Go, go now! I'm going after dad!" The men slid into the water quickly and swam back with the information.

"John, good luck. I'll see you back on the ship," Charlie said as he headed into the water.

"Are you serious?" John said in an angry whisper.

"You should come, too."

"That's our father, you prick."

"Your father, not mine."

"Whatever, tell them that I'm going after him, and that things are status quo. Attack as usual. I need no reinforcement."

"What?" Charlie said as he took off his mask.

"Yeah, get outta here," John grasped his knife tightly and started to crawl off into the bush.

"Wait, hang on . . . ," Charlie joined his brother. Not too long after, the two brothers buried themselves in the sand, under the cover of the bush. Japanese walked around them, searching and ready to kill. Charlie looked at his brother with a look of fear and disdain. John motioned for him to stay down, and Charlie ducked his head further down into the brush. They both watched as the Japanese dragged their father blindfolded to an unknown location. They watched until he was no longer in sight.

John slowly crawled closer to Charlie as the Japanese walked all around them with guns ready to fire. John got close enough to Charlie, and then whispered into his ear.

"Alright look, we need to take out a straggler, make a silent knife kill, get his weapon, then move forward to the next guy. Just stay low. I'll get the first one." Charlie nodded yes in agreement. They both waited and watched as the Japanese scouted the area for more Americans. Ten minutes passed, and then the time came. A soldier was isolated from the group, and was only feet from where the men were covered up. John waited until the Japanese soldier's back was turned. He sprung up like a stalking lion and killed the man with a slice across his throat. He dragged the enemy into the bush, took off all of the man's clothes and put them on himself. He strapped the man's pack on himself, then silently covered his body as Charlie watched in horror. John took the automatic weapon off of the man, and laid down. The bush was clear ahead, so he motioned to Charlie to move forward. Charlie was frozen in fear, unable to move. John motioned and gave his little brother a look of confidence and urgency that cut through Charlie's fear, enabling Charlie to move. They crawled silently through the bush, one drag of the arm after another. They did this until they reached a sandy clearing, flanked on the right by an outcropping of rock. Straight forward was where they last saw their father, being taken into the hills of the island. They laid motionless for a few minutes at the edge of the bush, waiting for the right time to make their move. Just when they saw their window of opportunity, another isolated Japanese soldier strolled the edge with gun in hand. Charlie motioned to John that he would take him, by pointing to himself, then pointing to the soldier, then running his finger across his throat in a slitting motion. John hesitated, then nodded yes.

Charlie waited, his heart was pounding out of his chest, sweat ran down his brow, and adrenaline pumped through his body. All of a sudden he felt invincible. He slowly made it to his feet, never taking his eye off of the pacing soldier. He stood with power, hid behind a thick palm on the edge of the bush, and waited for his moment. The moment came, and without hesitation he moved like lightning, covered the man's mouth then slit his throat. He quickly pulled the man into the bush. He looked at John in a dream state with empty eyes, then made focus. He did just as his brother did, and they were now masked as Japanese soldiers. Their tan skin, brown eyes, and sharp yet rounded faces made them look very Japanese. The two laid in the bush, and whispered ever so quietly to one another.

"What the hell's next, big bro? We're obviously not Japs . . . and what if our own shoot us?" Charlie asked into his brother's ear.

"They won't have a chance to shoot us. We're going now, and by the time our men have landed we'll be back with dad, alright. Do you remember our Japanese lessons?"

"Yeah."

"Be ready to use them. We're scouts returning to base, can you say that? Huh?" Charlie nodded yes. "Alright, good. And, if they're on to us, then we stab them, alright?"

"Right."

"Alright, let's move," John said with confidence. They moved in silence, standing straight up. They walked at a regular pace straight towards where their father was taken.

"This is crazy, John," Charlie said under his breath as they walked.

"Yeah, it is. Just keep walking."

"They're looking at us, you know that, right?" Charlie said.

"Maybe."

"This is stupid."

"Just trust me, brother, we're just one of them."

The two walked and then nonchalantly found cover among some trees and thick bush.

"John, what the hell are we doing?"

"I don't know, I just know dad's up in that area. Nobody's come after us yet, so let's just roll with it."

"So what, we're just gonna walk in there and tell them that we need to take the prisoner for a walk? That's nuts."

"Charlie, I don't know, let's just remain unseen, and get as close to where they have him as possible, o.k.?"

"Whatever, I just don't want to interact with any of these jokers. My Japanese only goes so far, and that's pretty short. I don't want to talk to one single soul, got it."

"Alright, we'll stay low. We're gonna make it, alright, we'll wait until morning . . . as soon as our infantry is on the ground, and the battle is in full swing--then we'll make our move."

"Won't that be too late? Imagine what they could do to him in just those hours."

"And you care?"

"I'm here, aren't I? I could be safe on the ship . . . instead I'm dressed in this monkey suit with a kill on my belt. So, shut up, John."

"O.k., o.k., I'm sorry. So what do you suggest?"

"I say we do like you said in the first place. We'll crawl our way up to the old man. Then when we get there, we'll see what's goin' on. If he's about to die, we make a move; if not, then we'll wait for the calvary as cover."

"O.k., alright, let's crawl."

Charlie and John commando crawled their way along for the next hour. They made their way under a half moon to the place where the Japanese held their father captive. It was well guarded, and they stayed hidden, just watching.

"Now what?" Charlie whispered as they lied in the bushes.

"We wait until dawn . . . or a lull. More than likely there's at least eight men on guard of that site, for now. And we have no idea how they have him contained. More than likely they're interrogating him."

"Uh, you think? He could be dead by morning. I don't care if he wasn't there for me, or what, he's part of our team. We gotta move in," Charlie said quietly, very close to his brother's ear as they both laid there in the bush.

"O.k., we have to be patient at the same time, though, alright?"

"Alright."

The brothers waited and watched, studying the movement, analyzing the situation. There were two armed guards standing watch at the entrance of the cave. The entrance was blocked by an iron gate, and they could see the keys dangling from one of the Japanese guards. The guards would talk, laugh at times, and smoke. They could hear talking, then yelling, then yelps from what they only could imagine was their father being interrogated and undergoing severe torture.

"Alright, we have to move," John said.

"Yeah, but what do you suggest we do? Those dudes look mean, and there's iron bars."

"We get to a position where we can get up. We walk up with these Japanese cigs in our mouth, and pretend like we need lights from the guards. They'll each oblige and when their hands are free we stab them in their carotids. They'll fall, I'll drag mine off quickly, then you yours, then we'll be the new guards. We shoulder their weapons, too."

"You are crazy."

"I guess. It's now, or dad dies, right?"

"Maybe."

"You said it yourself. Do you have any other ideas?"

"I mean, probably, but I can't think of any. Then what? We're guards and then we open the gate nonchalantly, and start blasting."

"Yeah, but we'll have to make mainly silent kills, and then blast our way out on to the beach, and swim back to the ship, with dad."

"You make it sound like this is a walk in the park. What about the high watches. They'll see us taking out the guards."

"Maybe, maybe not. This is pretty hidden. They're probably jawing away and whatever, waiting to fight anyhow."

"They already know we're here John, c'mon man. They're looking all around right now."

"Then we have to do it fast."

"And if someone inside sees that we've just killed the guard?"

"Alright, let's maneuver to get better info on what's beyond the bars, and let's scope the high sights. We've got binoculars, right here."

"Alright."

The mission, nearly impossible; the will, however, made it possible. They scoped out the sights, and after careful consideration deemed the plan viable. The cave that was being used as a prison was well guarded, with well-armed men, but it was hidden away from most peering eyes.

"Alright, you ready?" John asked.

"No, but . . ."

"O.k., let's scoot over there, then slowly make our way to our feet.

Get a cig in your mouth, slant those eyes, and smile, alright?"

"Yeah, alright."

The two crawled then slowly stood up unnoticed. They walked up to the guards just as sure as sure could be. They pretended to be talking to one another, and then pulled up to the guards, cigs in mouth, slanted eyes and big smiles.

"Where are you jokers headed?" one of the guard's asked in Japanese. John smiled even bigger, and just nodded up, then pointed to his cigarette.

"Light?" John said in Japanese. Charlie did the same and at the same time they were both getting their cigarettes lit. And, in a flash, they both stabbed the soldiers in their throats. Both men fell, and both were quickly caught then dragged out of sight. They took turns dragging, as the other paced with their back to the entrance, smoking a cigarette. After both of the Japanese soldiers were hidden away, and the brothers had the keys in hand they just stood watch, playing the part of guards.

Charlie looked at John with a look of fear, and John mirrored it right back. They both listened and on occasion caught a glimpse into the mouth of a cave system. Only thirty feet stood between them and their father. There were three armed soldiers, and an interrogator pressing their father.

"Tell us now, and we'll let you go," they heard the interrogator say in English.

"I swear to God, they don't tell us these things. They just give orders, and mine was to scout the beach, that's all," Panther said very nasally, as if his nose had been broken. "It's because of this, they don't tell us anything."

"Oh, is that right? Well, what did your little scouts see?"

"I don't know. I was taken before I could find out."

"O.k., o.k., so you don't know anything. You are a liar, and I despise liars. Now tell me, do you value your life, because if you don't tell me anything, well then you are good for nothing, and I will kill you. I rather enjoy killing liars. So, what's it going to be, huh? Huh!" the soldier digs his gun into Panther's temple and forces his head to the table. "How about a little bit of encouragement," the soldier motions to another soldier, and instantly the soldier takes Panther's right hand, pins it down to the table, and drives his knife through his hand with downward force and pins it to the table. Panther lets out a cry. "So, now, tell me, when is the attack, how many soldiers, and what is your strategy?"

"I don't know."

"O.k. good, because I wanted to kill you anyways."

John pulled the keys out, unlocked the door, and the two walk slowly into the prison. No one noticed until they were close.

"What are you two doing? Stand guard!" one soldier yelled in Japanese. John searched for the right response, for the right Japanese.

"We want to watch," John said as he and Charlie stood among the three. The interrogator turned and looked at the men, all eager to watch.

"Well o.k. then! This is good! But then right back to your posts!" the man pulled the hammer back on his gun, and that's when John quickly took aim, fired and killed the interrogator. Charlie quickly dropped to his knees and opened up machine gun fire on the midsections of the three soldiers, killing two, and the other took aim as he was falling. John turned and shot the soldier in the head. John quickly takes the knife from his father's hand and lifts him up. He showed his face, and then he said "run!" to his brother and dad. And run they did. Panther grabbed a fallen machine gun, and they tore out of there at break-neck speed. The shots were heard and it quickly brought attention from deeper within the network of caves. They were quickly pursued, as well as quickly cut off, once they hit the opening that lied between the caves and the bush. John, Charlie, and Panther opened fire on unsuspecting soldiers, killing all that were in front of them. They ran like deer through the brush, taking an alternate route to the sea. As soon as they reached the water bullets were flying by their heads, as they all dove in. Just as they entered the water a bullet pierced John's leg. They all went underwater and didn't come up for four minutes, swimming as deep as they could as bullets whizzed by them under the moonlit water. Blood poured from both John's wounded leg, as well as his father's hand. Sharks from hundreds of yards started to make their way to the scent, as well as the movement. They swam for their ship. The only time they came up for air was in a manner that only allowed their mouths to surface, then it was back down. Panther stopped John and Charlie while they were ten feet deep underwater. He motioned John to take off his Japanese pants. He did, quickly. Panther took out his knife, cut off the pant legs and made a tourniquet above John's wound, and then wrapped the wound itself to slow the bleeding. Panther tied his own hand up and secured the remains of the pants around his own leg, so they didn't float up. They went up, only with their mouths for air, and then kept swimming underwater.

They were nearing the ships, when they came upon UDT about to set and detonate underwater explosives on to the reef. The crew drew their knives, unsure as to who the men were, especially with two of them dressed in Japanese uniform. Panther swam ahead fast, as to show his face. Within a few seconds they had recognition, as well as recognition of the two others, John and Charlie. They also took notice to the trail of blood that led to two hungry, lurking Tiger sharks. The looks upon the detonation squad told the story, as their faces turned to horror.

"Sharks!" the one UDT said and bubbles came out of his mouth as he was only able to mouth the word. Panther, John, and Charlie all turned around to see the oncoming sharks. Two men swam quickly towards the sharks while the men finished placing the mines. They carried high powered harpoons and were ready to face the sharks head on. The one, more aggressive of the two, sharks headed straight for John. The soldier fired his harpoon and made a direct hit into the body of the shark . . . but the shark kept going. Panther swam directly at the shark as it charged his son, and frantically stabbed at it, aiming for the eyes and brain. The other harpoon swimmer positioned himself beneath the shark and fired his harpoon directly into its throat. The harpoon penetrated, and came out the other side, which was the top of the Tiger's neck. Panther quickly pulled his knife away and swam to John. All of the divers went slowly up for air, all the while watching the second shark. The second shark saw a free meal and began devouring the dead shark, and other smaller sharks joined in on the feeding frenzy. The men circled around John and they all swam underwater to the ship.

Once aboard they were met by an infuriated captain, and a medic.

"What the holy hell were you boys thinking?! Damn it soldiers! I ought to throw you three in the brig! What happened out there? No, don't tell me, I'm too pissed to wanna know! Do you know how much you compromised our mission?! Huh, do you? Don't talk! Get these men taken care of, and I will talk to you two in my office after you clean up!"

"Yes, sir!" the two said as they stood at attention and John lay on the deck of the ship.

"Are those explosives ready?" the captain asked the rest of the men, who were also standing at attention, dripping wet.

"Yes sir!" they said in unison.

"Well, blast 'em for God sake, what are you waiting for?! We've got a battle to fight!"

"Yes, sir!"

John and Wes were taken to the infirmary to have their wounds treated. Charlie showered in a state of shock, stress, and trauma. He could hardly believe it was all real, and was waiting to wake up. He let the hot water rain on his twitching muscles as he recounted the events, like a horrible nightmare. He was overcome with emotions, and he slid down to the floor. He wanted to cry, but there were no tears. The emotions were locked, emotions of old, gray and suppressed wanting to surface but were unable to. The emotions of killing men were present, and there was no place for them to go. So, these new emotions got pushed further down, and were just waiting to explode with all of the others.

Charlie got dressed and met the captain in his office.

"Captain, sir," Charlie said and saluted.

"At ease." Charlie sat down. "Now I'm fully aware of what you and your brother did for your father . . . or should I say fellow UDT. The men swam back with the reconnaissance information, and told me what you two were up to. Now, first thing's first. You two broke protocol. You're aware of that, are you not?"

"Yes, sir."

"We would have been seriously compromised if all three of you were taken captive. Do you realize that?"

"Yes, sir. But with all due respect sir, I don't know that much."

"You know enough, that's for sure."

"Yes, sir."

"When a prisoner is taken we form battalions of blood-thirsty marines to retrieve them, not two unarmed swimmers. That being said, good work. Both you and your brother will be up for the medals of honor. What you and your brother did goes above and beyond. And more than I am pissed, I am proud, son."

"Yes sir, thank you, sir. It's John you should be praising, not me. I just followed him."

"Well, when I get a chance I will. But make sure this is very clear, and I'll tell your brother the same thing . . . if you ever pull that crap again you'll be on k.p. until your hands shrivel up and die."

"Yes, sir."

"And while we're at it, I'm going to need a detailed description of every last thing that you saw. You were in a prison?"

"Yes, sir, of sorts. It was a mouth to a network of tunnels. John sent the swimmers back with sights and layout, after our father was taken. I didn't want to stay, and John wasn't leaving either way. So, I joined him. We crawled through the bush, covered ourselves up with sand and leaves. We waited for the right time, and then John took a soldier . . . knife kill . . . silent as a breeze. He dragged him into the bush, took off all of the soldier's clothes, put them on himself and then took his machine gun off of him. It was my turn next. I waited, and then made the kill. I did the same as John . . . and then we were both dressed as Japs."

"You don't say."

"Yes, sir. Then we crawled even further, got close to their cave imprisonment, which is on the right flank of the island within an outcropping of rocks. It runs deep. There were two guards, well hidden from snipers, and John hatched the plan to walk up to them as a couple of Japs needing our cigs lit . . . I thought it was crazy, but he saw that they held the keys to the gate. So, we walked up to them, John said "fire" in Japanese, I did the same, and as they lit our cigs, we stabbed them in the throats. I stood as a Jap guard, while John dragged the bodies off. Then we heard them interrogating Wes, and he wasn't budging. We heard him scream, we looked and his hand was pinned to the table by a knife. They were about to execute him, and that's when we went in. We pretended like we wanted to watch, and just as they were about to shoot him, John shot the Jap in the back. I dropped to my knees and opened automatic fire on three Japs, killing two. The third lifted his gun to shoot me, and John shot him. We freed my dad from the knife, and then other Japs from the tunnel chased after us, and we went out guns blazing. Wes had an automatic, too, and we took out another four or five Japs before we reached the bush. We sprinted to the water and dove in. That's when John took a bullet to the leg. We swam underwater, John was bleeding, Wes made him a tunicate under water, and then the sharks came. Two UDT's setting mines shot the one, and my dad stabbed at its head. The other tiger shark started to eat the dead one, and then a bunch of sharks showed up. All of the swimmers made a circle around John, and we all swam to the ship."

"Well, I'll be damned. Did I say proud? That doesn't quite cut it now, does it?"

"I'm not sure sir," Charlie hung his head.

"Keep that chin up son, you did the right thing. Now, if you don't mind, I've got a war to fight. You're dismissed."

"Sir, yes sir," Charlie rose and saluted the captain then left his office.

6

CHARLIE HEADED OVER TO THE INFIRMARY AFTER GATHERING HIS thoughts and composure.

"Hey John, how's that leg?" he said as he stood by his bed. The sun was just rising and the sounds of war were just beginning.

"It's alright. How's your head?"

"Huh?"

"You know, that was some heavy stuff. I'm sorry I dragged you into it."

"You didn't drag me. It's called free will, John . . . and, well, I wouldn't abandon you or dad."

"Yeah, well thanks, you gotta lotta guts, little bro."

"Yeah, you too."

"Why don't you go over there and talk to dad. He's been asking all about you . . . he's worried, you know."

"About what?" Charlie asked.

"About you . . . about your heart . . . about your pain, and now, on top of all that, what you just went through."

"Oh, yeah, well, this train doesn't slow down now, does it?"

"So, are you going to talk to him or what? Ahhh . . ."

"What is it?"

"It's just a little pain. Hey get that nurse for me, on your way over to dad, alright?"

"This coming from a devoted man."

"Hey, it's not like I'm gonna grope her or anything."

"Yeah, alright. Looks like I can still outrun you . . . after all these years," Charlie smiled at John.

"Yep, otherwise your ass would be laying here. So, go on, get the nurse, and talk to dad. He loves you, just like I do."

"Yeah, I'll get the nurse for you," Charlie said as he turned and walked away.

"Hey, Charlie, you did good," John said loudly to Charlie's back. Charlie just raised his hand as he walked towards the nurse. He reached her, put his hand on the small of her back, then spoke.

"Hey, my brother thinks you're really cute, and he wants you to give him a shot in his rear end. I told him that you were way out of his league, but . . . he said that it was worth a shot anyhow, no pun intended, really," Charlie smiled at the pretty nurse as she looked over at John, who just waved. Then Charlie eyed his dad, resting with his hand wrapped up in a bandage. He walked slowly up to him, with his head down, and then lifted it. Panther was waiting, anticipating, and as Charlie lifted his head, Panther made eye contact with his son. And, in that moment, he saw his little baby boy.

"Hey, how's the hand?" Charlie said as he stood by his father's bed side.

"Could be worse, I guess. They managed to cut just through my flesh, and nothing else, so . . . I guess that's good. How are you?"

"O.k.," Charlie said with pain in his eyes.

"It's o.k. not to be o.k. Charlie. I'm not o.k."

"Yeah, well, I'm o.k . . . .messed up, but o.k. I'm alive anyhow."

"Yeah. That was the bravest and kindest act a man could bestow upon another. You saved my life. You and John . . . who'd a thought, I was the one coming for you. And here I am, alive, with my boys, and you two are my heroes. You have always been. You have always been my inspiration, my reason for living, and I just want you to know Charlie . . ." Panther's emotions started to rise, and he choked up a little bit, while fighting back tears. "I just want you to know that I love you. I love you so much. And there's not a day that goes by that I don't think about that day in the woods. It haunts me; it haunts me in my sleep. It haunts me while my eyes are wide open. And I wish that I would have just kept running. I would have ran, I would have killed, and I would have kept us together . . . even if it meant us dying. At least . . . at least . . . we would have been together," Panther's tears became unstoppable, and he grabbed Charlie's hand with his good hand. "I just hope that you can . . . someday . . . forgive me." A tear rolled down Charlie's face, as he looked his father in the eyes.

"Well uh, ya know, it's been more than any person should have to go through . . . but, dad, you don't have to wait for forgiveness. I forgive you now. I forgave you on that beach when Japanese blood spilled right in front of me, by my own hand." Just then a siren went off for all men to assume their battle positions. "Shoot, hah," Charlie smiled slightly, as he wiped his tear. "It looks like we're all gonna get to die together after all." Charlie gripped his dad's hand and then started to run out of the infirmary.

"Hey, where you going?!" John yelled from his bed.

"Where do you think? I'm gonna see if the captain will put me on one of those big guns! I'm not gonna let those Japs sink this ship, not with you two on it!" Charlie sprinted out, and instead of assuming his battle station, which for UDT's was just to bunker down, he went to the captain himself asking for further duty.

"Captain, sir. Permission to take arms, sir!"

"For God sake soldier, haven't you had enough! Can't you see I'm busy here?" Enemy planes were circling, and firing at the ships, at the men, in the thousands, as they stormed the island.

"Sir, no sir. Let me on a big hitter, I wanna kill some Japs, sir."

"Son, you can't man those weapons, you're out of your mind. But, go into my quarters, and get a machine gun from my case. You have permission to fire on planes. Go!"

Charlie tore out of there like a bat out of hell, grabbed a machine gun, and a large box of ammo. He set up on a flank near a gunner, and started shooting down planes. A kamikaze was about a half mile out, headed straight for their port side of the ship. The gunner yelled out as the plane leveled out only feet from the water on a direct course. Charlie unloaded a hundred rounds at the front window, causing the pilot to lose control as the wing tilted sharply towards the water and then the gunner shot a massive round that took the plane out. It crashed only a hundred feet from the ship, exploding into a fiery ball of flames. Then another one was in route, right behind it. Charlie and the gunner let their rounds fly, and blew the plane up mid-air.

"Yeah!" Charlie yelled with adrenaline pumping throughout his body.

"Nice shootin' froggie!" the gunner yelled with a smile. "Don't stop now, there's more of where that came from. Straight ahead, enemy plane!"

Charlie started unloading rounds, and with each bullet a piece of his pain was released towards the enemy. Memories of abuse flashed through his mind as he squeezed the trigger. He pictured all of the people, kids, adults, foster parents, teachers, bullies and anyone else whoever made his life Hell, right there in the cockpits of the planes. He screamed with raging release as he took out plane after plane. He moved from one side of the ship to the other, bow to stern, port to starboard, with hazed over eyes, unloading round after round on the enemy.

The ship, after deploying all of its troops, maneuvered its position back and away to avoid enemy fire on both the ship, and the storming troops. The ships behind followed suite, and they all moved in an octagonal shape, keeping the most vital ships in the middle. Charlie went for more ammo, and kept firing on enemy planes as John and Wes stayed below, recovering from their wounds. Men kept pouring into the infirmary with bullet wounds, filling up beds, demanding much attention.

"Hey John, so, how's that girl of yours?" Wes asked as he walked over to John's bedside.

"Some time for a conversation, dad," John said as the boat surged, and war raged.

"Yeah, well, that's kind of why I'm over here, John."

"Oh, were getting out of here dad, don't you worry about that."

"Oh yeah, I know, but I just wanted to let you know, just in case, you know, anything happens, that I love you John . . . I love you Lakota," Panther takes his son by his hand, trying not to lose his balance.

"I know you do, dad."

"You know, I don't know what you two went through all of those years, and I know it's not the best time to talk about it, but . . ." Panther paused, then spoke louder over all of the noise. "I just want you to know how sorry I am. And if this is our last chance to talk, then I just want you to know how proud of you that I am. You have become an exceptional man, and I'm so proud to be your father."

"O.k. dad, I know, dad. But, hey, we'll have plenty of time to talk about this later, o.k.?" John gives his dad a little smile.

"O.k."

"I wonder what Charlie's up to?"

"I don't know." Just then a massive explosion went off. A submarine successfully struck the ship with a torpedo. The sirens went off, and the nurses quickly prepared the twenty injured men, the other eighteen came in one by one, each with bullets wounds, for evacuation.

"I'm going after my son!" Wes yelled at the nurse, but was abruptly stopped by a seaman with a gun.

"There's no way!" He yelled, and Wes looked back at John with a look of great despair, and horror. "The whole front of the ship is blown up, we're going down fast! We need to get all of these men out onto life boats, now!" Wes rushed to John's side and helped him out of bed. John ripped out his I.V., and hobbled along with his dad in agonizing pain. Men rushed by to assist the wounded onto the deck. When John and Wes surfaced they saw the horror, and panic, and the chaos.

"Do you see Charlie!" Wes yelled above the roar of war and destruction all around them.

"No! I can't see anything, dad!"

"Alright, c'mon, onto the boat!" Once aboard with the other wounded, they were lowered into the water. Men were bleeding from their wounds, moaning from the pain, and lack of morphine. John looked around in disbelief as men screamed in the water, blown in half from the explosion, desperately trying to stay afloat and avoid the inevitable. Men screaming to God, men screaming for help, men dying in the water all around their life boat.

"We've got to help them!" John yelled as a man tried to swim towards the boat in a pool of blood. He tried to yell for help, but was cut short as a shark violently ripped into his side and pulled him under the water. "No!" John screamed.

"John, John, c'mon, stay with me, hey, stay with me," Panther said as he grabbed John's arm, knowing that John was about to dive in after the screaming men.

"Charlie! It's Charlie! Charlie, what the hell are you doing!" John screamed as he spotted his brother swimming after wounded soldiers who were immersed in a crimson sea. "Charlie!" John screamed but was unheard. John and his father watched as Charlie dragged a man to a boat as sharks ripped apart wounded soldiers. They watched as he dragged them to safety, then went back for more. Their own boat was on an expedited course for the nearest ship to take care of the boat full of wounded soldiers.

"It's o.k. John, it's o.k. He's gonna make it," Wes said as they neared another ship.

"We should have gone in after him . . . we should have gone in too . . . after those men . . . ," John hung his head.

"We would have been dead in the water, John. I can't swim, nor can you. Charlie's strong, he will make it. Do you hear me John . . . hey, hey . . ." Wes grabbed his son by his shoulders then lifted his chin. "He's gonna make it."

Panther and Lakota were hauled aboard a naval ship, and immediately treated. They were among hundreds wounded in battle. They laid in their cots just waiting for another attack. Men screamed as they came in with the most gruesome injuries one could imagine.

Limbs blown off, faces shot off, guts spilling out, fragments of explosives sticking out of skulls, and all John could do was look for Charlie. He prayed he'd see him wounded not dead; he prayed that he'd just see him again.

"Dad!" John yelled from his bed. Panther was among the walking wounded and came to his bed side.

"What is it?"

"Find Dakota."

"Huh?"

"Find him."

"He could be anywhere, it's not that I don't want to, I just don't know where or how. We're moving out, this ship is moving out."

"We can't leave him dad! I don't care if I die trying to find him. We've come this far together." John started to roll over and tried to sit up on to his leg, but the pain was too excruciating.

"We're not, Lakota, he's o.k. We'll see him again. I know it."

"How do you know? What the hell do you know that I don't? Huh?"

"I just know. We'll see him soon."

"Yeah, in a box! How can you be so calm?! Damn it! What's your problem, dad! He's your son!"

"I know, Lakota, but what am I supposed to do? Take a boat out into the middle of nowhere? We're miles away now."

"Yes, go, go now. Search the ship, there's gotta be another sick bay. Go!"

"O.k., o.k. John, I'll look, alright. I want him here just as much as you do . . . maybe more. Don't forget that, you both are my sons, you both are my heart."

"Then go! And while you're at it, tell the nurse to give me some of what you got, what is that, valium? Damn!"

"O.k., o.k. I'll be right back."

Panther hurried out of there and asked around for another sick bay. He found out rather quickly that there were two other sick bays and so he rushed to the first. He went in, nearly lost his balance on a slick of blood, and the sight nearly made him pass out. It was far worse in this unit. Surgery was taking place on sight, men were moaning in pain, blood and puke were everywhere, as nurses scurried about.

"What are you doing in here?" a nurse asked as she wiped up the blood at Panther's feet.

"I'm looking for someone. Charlie Morrison?"

"Good luck, you'll have to go to each bed and look at all of the men's faces, and tags. But I'll tell you what, you can't be in here . . . not now. Just pray your friend is in sick bay two or three."

"O.k., o.k." Panther quickly scanned the faces, but could only see shadows, backs of heads, blood, doctors, nurses, and not one single recognizable face. He turned and ran out.

"Hey soldier, where the hell are you going in such a hurry?" a commanding officer said as he stopped Panther in his tracks.

"I'm going back to sick bay, sir."

"Good. Carry on."

Panther ran to sick bay three with the angst and urgency that he'd felt for the last twenty odd years. He entered in to the sick bay, and it was much more like his own sick bay, less intense, but still bloody and awful. He walked up and down the bed lines, looking for his son.

"Hey, old man, over here!" Charlie called out with a loopy smile.

"Charlie! Oh my God, thank you. Charlie!" Panther said as he rushed to his son's side.

"Thought I was a goner, huh?!" Charlie joked as he laid with his side heavily bandaged.

"No, I mean, we were sure hoping not," Panther rested his hand on Charlie's arm and smiled as he looked him in the eyes.

"Yeah, well, it was close alright. But hey, I'm here, and I did my job."

"We saw you, from the life raft, what you did was beyond brave . . . more courage than I've ever seen in a man."

"Yeah, and before that I was hunting planes like ducks," he said with a little smile from the morphine.

"So, what happened? Is it bad?"

"No, no, just a shark bite . . . I felt that son of a bitch as soon as he tried to bite into me. It was on the way to a man in the water; he was the real mess, blood everywhere. He got his arm and side of his face blown off in the explosion. Sharks were tearing into bodies all around, and he was the last one I got in."

"So, the shark got you?"

"Not really . . . I stabbed it as soon as I felt its teeth go into my side. So the poor shark only got a taste then let go. But when they taste, they don't lick."

"So, how deep are your wounds?"

"The med said that the teeth went in about a half inch, right in my side, halfway up into my ribs. I was lucky it didn't thrash, and rip out the flesh, then I'd be a goner. It just clamped, I stabbed, then it let go. I swam for the guy, quickly got him to a life boat, and here we are now . . . alive," he weakly smiled, then coughed from talking, and then winced from the pain.

"Here, let me get you some water."

"Make that a vodka tonic dad." They shared a smile and Panther came back with some water.

"Here you go. So John is awful worried about you. I should get back and let him know you're alive."

"Yeah, o.k. I'll be here, I'm not going anywhere. Tell him no little shark's gonna take out the kid from Kansas."

"O.k., I will."

"Hey, maybe we'll get a break, all three of us being mangled like we are," Charlie smiled.

"Yeah, maybe."

The wounded were flown home to the states on temporary leave from the military. They were taken to a San Diego naval base to recuperate, and then when ready they were to be redeployed. They were all near the end of their recoveries, and were feeling much better after only a few weeks of rest. They were given a two-day R&R, and so John had Sarah fly in for those two short days. She arrived Friday evening, and then took a taxi to a club where John, Charlie, and Wes were going to meet her at eight o'clock.

"C'mon John, what are you doing in there, man? You need to just pinch it bro, this is going to be a big night for you man!" Charlie said outside John's bathroom door.

"I know! Hang on, I've got diarrhea! It had to be tonight!" he yelled from inside then smashed the door with his hand in frustration. Charlie just stepped backed and laughed a little.

"What's going on?"

"Wouldn't you like to know, Wes."

"What, what is it?"

"He's got the runs. And he's supposed to be smooching up his little lady right now!" Charlie said louder to the door.

"Screw off, Charlie!"

"It's already eight twenty, man. She's waiting there, and you're crapping here."

"Just go on without me. Get the picture out of my wallet, and find her."

"I'm not doing that."

"Why?"

"Because . . . I don't know . . . just get it all out of you, and then we'll go. She's a big girl; she'll be alright."

"Alright . . . what are you looking at, let's go."

"Yes, that's what I'm talking about . . . I'm getting some tonight!"

"Hey, hey, is that any way to talk around your father?"

"No, but on the battlefield, in my head, and tonight . . . you are Wes. Yes, you are my dad, but dad, Wes, I, Charlie, A.K.A. Dakota, need some action . . . is that o.k. with you?" Panther didn't know what to say, so he just laughed.

"O.k., but don't make me a grandfather. I'm just trying to get back into the swing of being a father."

"Oh, don't you worry about me," Charlie said as they all walked out, John with a slight limp still, supporting himself with a cane.

"Let's just hope your girl can still love a man with a limp," Charlie said and winked at John.

"Yeah, well, good thing it's the only limp thing I got going on. I am strong like bull," John said with a funny accent and a wink back to his little brother.

They showed up to the night club, and John's heart was racing with anticipation. It was packed with soldiers on R&R, as well as local folks. The place was jumpin' with big band music, guys and girls dancing and drinking. It was full of energy. John scanned the room with his dad and brother on each side.

"See her?" Charlie asked as he looked around too.

"No, not yet, c'mon."

They searched the place over, with no sign of her. So, John, with his family by his side, asked around. He asked anyone and everyone. Then he made it to the bartender.

"Hey, you haven't seen a pretty brunette girl in here? Greenish blue eyes girl, next door kind of woman. She came in alone, and I'm supposed to meet her here."

"Man, I see a lot of girls in here. Anything more specific?" the bartender asked, as he remained busy serving drinks.

"She said she would wear a red hat and red dress . . . just so I wouldn't miss her."

"Well, now, hang on. She came in alone huh?"

"Yep."

"You know now that I think about it, about an hour ago, a pretty young girl came in here, alone, just like you say, with a red dress and hat. A real looker, huh?"

"You could say that."

"Yeah, she was at the bar actually, then she went off to the bathroom I suppose, because she was refusing guys to dance left and right."

"Alright, thanks. C'mon guys." John's heart pounded even harder with worry.

"Maybe she's out front, and we missed her." John hoped.

"Yeah, alright, let's check." Both his dad and brother followed.

They all went out front to have a look. Each one of them looked, but saw nothing. Then they went around the side towards the side of the building, and that's when John heard her voice. He ran as fast as he could, using his cane as his third leg. Charlie and Panther followed close behind.

"Get off of me!" Sarah yelled, and only John, his brother, and his father could hear her screams. A man had her pinned against the wall, forcing himself upon her. Another man stood and watched. They were both in military uniform, and both clueless to the rushing men. Charlie was on scene first, and in a full sprint tackled the man watching. Panther was right behind him in a sprint as well, and he did the same, blindsiding the soldier who was about to rape Sarah. John was next on scene and quickly grabbed Sarah. He put her behind him, and then watched as a fury was unleashed on the unsuspecting men. Charlie had pinned the one man, smashing his face in with ferocious power and anger, while Panther, with the same, if not more rage, hammered the face and head of the rapist with his one good hand. Sarah whimpered, and John put his hand back to hers to hold.

"O.k., o.k., I'm sorry!" the guy Panther had pinned down screamed.

"Say it again!"

"I'm sorry, just let me go! I swear, I'm sorry!" Just then the guy Charlie had pinned, gained control, and rolled on top of Charlie. That's when John saw the knife in the guy's hand. John ran without pain, in an adrenaline rush, towards the knife, pulled out his own. That's when the world stood still. And as the guy went to stab Charlie, John stabbed the soldier in the back of his neck, severing his spinal cord, killing him instantly. He fell limp onto Charlie. John looked up in shock, and saw the same shock in everyone else's eyes. He looked up to a terrified Sarah. Charlie pushed the man's body off of him. The soldier was a celebrated, white, Chief Officer.

"Oh my God, what do we do?" John asked as he held his bloody knife. Panther was still sitting on the other guy, a Senior Chief Officer.

"We run," Panther said as he turned back, and knocked the soldier out with a strong punch to the head.

"What?" John asked with an adrenalized quiver in his voice.

"The color of your skin is going to put you away, John, for a very long time. There's no neutral witnesses here. We run."

"Yeah, John, I'm not gonna stand witness against you, no way," Charlie said as he wiped blood from his face.

"We can't run. We'll get a fair trial. There's no way we're running, they'll believe Sarah," John said with despair as he looked up at Sarah.

"They're right John. This guy's gonna wake up and they'll believe him over you guys, even me."

"Oh my God, alright. Let's run. Tie him up, dad, use his own belt." Panther tied the knocked out soldier up, and they ran. They hailed a cab to Sarah's hotel, and hid out in the room for only a few minutes.

"We have to cross the border, tonight. We need to take off our navy clothes, get into street clothes, and cross in a cab as tourists," Panther said.

"I don't know, dad, I don't think I can do this. No, I can't. I can't put you all through this, no way. Not Sarah, not you guys, no way. I'm gonna stand up to this, I have to," John said in disarray.

"John, Lakota, listen to me," Panther said as he knelt down and got John to look him in the eyes. "You will never see Sarah again. Not until you are an old man anyways. I can't lose you again. All the jury is gonna see is your color. The man you killed was a very high ranked, well respected officer, and his buddy too. You will be charged with murder, and you will be put away for a very long time. Hey, listen, you defended your brother, you saved his life, and now it's time to go. Do you hear me? I won't let you go. Do you hear me?

131

You're gonna have to get passed me, and I'm not afraid to knock you out. I'll drag you to Mexico."

"Yeah, me too," Charlie agreed. "I won't let you turn yourself in, no way."

"Well, Sarah, you should go," John said in tears as he lifted his head. "You don't have anything to do with this. They'll never find you, just fly home."

"No way, John. I love you, and we're going."

"What about your family?"

"I'll call them and tell them that I'm joining the peace corp. I don't care."

"Oh my God, this isn't happening. I should have just cut his arm, or something . . . it was just like, I don't know. It went black, I saw them, and I . . . I messed up."

"It is happening and you didn't mess up. We need to go, now. Take off your tops, just t-shirts, and we go, now!" Panther said as he took off his, and Charlie did the same. Then they both helped take off John's, and helped him up. John looked everyone in their eyes, saw their love and readiness to support him. John stood on his cane, and they all hurried out to get a cab. They traveled for the next fifteen minutes or so.

"This is far enough," Charlie said to the cabbie.

"Huh?" Panther said.

"Trust me. This is where we want to eat," he gave them all an eye and a fake smile. They got out right before the border and walked to a small Mexican restaurant. They went inside.

"He would have driven us right in Charlie, what was that all about?" Panther asked as they sat down at a table.

"Won't they check our IDs? Do we need a passport? What? We

can't show any of that," Charlie said.

"They don't need any of that. The border is pretty loose. We just go in. So, c'mon, let's get another cab," Panther said.

"Are you sure?" Charlie questioned again.

"Yes, I'm sure, guys in the joint would talk about it. If you'd feel better, we can all just walk in. But it's a long walk for John."

"Alright, I didn't know."

"He's right Charlie. It's loose on the way in," John said. "But they might have a radio dispatch out on us by now, so let's just make the walk. We need disguises. I saw an open market with random stuff next door, let's go there."

"We're gonna have to make you look like an old man, with that leg of yours," Charlie said as they all walked quickly out of the room and to the elevator.

"Yeah."

They were able to find a general/thrift-like store still open as they hustled towards the border. Each one of them got busy, with deadly seriousness, buying clothes, hats, glasses, wigs and anything they could to disguise themselves for their walk into Mexico. All that they had was the money in their pockets, Sarah having more than all of them put together. She paid the clerk and they left.

They all walked down the street in disguise. John dressed in an old suit, a wispy gray wig, an old fart's hat, his cane and wore a gray mustache. Charlie just bought some regular street clothes, leaning towards the tourist look, and wore a hat as well as a pair of reading glasses. Panther did nearly the same, only he bought a full fake beard that stuck to his face. Sarah bought a simple dress, and a red haired wig. They moved as quickly as possible to the border.

"Just act natural, calm, o.k." Panther said as he looked around.

"You're one to talk," Charlie said as he looked at his dad.

"Right, o.k."

"As far as I'm concerned, I am finally free. I'm gonna start a new life, find a little Mexican girl, build a little hut on the beach and be a fisherman. And I owe it all to you John," Charlie said plainly, but with a little bit of enthusiasm.

"You're messing with me, right?" John asked as he hobbled along.

"No, man. You know what, I change my mind, me and Sarah are going to have to get together, I'm not too keen on Mexican girls," Charlie said with a smile and a wink for John. "I mean, you can't even keep up old man."

"Very funny, hey, wait up . . ." Charlie jokingly puts his arm around Sarah, and she looked back at John with a look of love for John and smiled—a smile he hadn't seen in too long. "Hey watch it there little bro, I can still whip you!" John said as he put his cane into overdrive and took Sarah off of his arm. "You're gonna get your own."

"What, am I livestock?" Sarah said as she leaned her head on John's shoulder.

"Yes, you're my livestock. Livestock that I love and cherish."

"Save it will ya," Charlie said and then put his arm around his dad.

"You guys are sure carrying on. It's like nothing ever happened," Panther said.

"Nothing did happen, and I thought you wanted us to relax . . . c'mon old man, tell me a joke."

"As soon as we get over this bridge, then I'd be glad to."

They all walked over the border, without a hitch, and were now officially in Mexico.

"O.k. now, how about that joke, ol' man?" Charlie said.

"Now's not the time, sorry Charlie, but we need to get lost."

134

7

Six months passed. Sarah's parents had received two letters, but were unable to respond. The group had moved steadily down the coast of Mexico living off of the land, and doing odd jobs along the way. They eventually drifted more inland into the mountainous region of the country with the goal of getting lost. And lost they were.

"I don't know about you guys, but I could really go for a hot shower," Charlie said as they walked into higher altitudes, thinner air, and intense sunlight. "I mean, don't get me wrong John, this has been great, I mean not having anything, on the run from the law, dreaming of the girls I could've had, eating whatever we've been eating," Charlie continued as they walked on sharp inclining paths forged by natives. He lagged behind with his walking stick in hand and spoke in a half joking, mainly cynical and sarcastic manner with labored breath. "The beach was nice. At least we should have gotten a donkey. I almost had enough money, just one more string of shells to stupid tourists and we might have had a nice ride up."

"Save your breath Charlie," John said, who had grown accustomed to Charlie's banter. "You know you can turn back if you'd like," John spoke loudly back to his brother.

"Yeah, maybe Alaska."

"Yep, then you could get a little Eskimo chick to make out with you in her igloo."

"Hey, will you guys quiet down. Don't you hear that? It's your shower, Charlie," Panther said, as he forged ahead of everyone. Everyone stopped and listened, listened very carefully.

"Huh, I don't hear anything," John said.

"Yeah ol' man, your hearing's goin' bad."

"No, no, I hear it," Sarah said as she wiped sweat from her head and looked at John with her aqua blue-green eyes that sparkled in the sunlight. "It's a water fall, or river, something."

"C'mon!" Panther said as he picked up his pace, and everyone else did as well. As they zig-zagged up the lush mountain side, the crashing of the waterfall started to become crystal clear in the ears of everyone. They started to run at this point, thirsty, dirty, exhausted, on the verge of hallucination, but still ran until they felt the mist, then all stopped in the wonderment of the massive sunlit waterfall that fell a hundred feet and crushed against solid rock. "Huh! Yee yee!" Panther broke the silence and ran to the river's edge.

"Whoa, whoa dad! Careful!" John was right on his tail.

"Yep!" Panther yelled back.

They all scurried about, taken by the magic and impending refreshment, trying to find a suitable place to get in. And within five minutes they did. A sparkling blue pool sat in perfection off to the side of the river only a hundred yards from the pounding waterfall. Charlie jumped in first, giving off a shout of joy. Panther followed with a giant splash. He swam over to Charlie and dunked his head in. Charlie popped back up with a smile and punched his dad in the jaw. Panther's face turned serious, then he saw the smile on Charlie's face.

"C'mon ol' man!" Charlie said as he invited a rumble.

"Oh no, you don't want a tussle this ol' man!" Panther said with a smile.

"Yeah I do! C'mon, right here, hit me right here, ol' man!" Panther smiled and then gave his son a jab to the chin.

"Woo hoo!" Charlie shouted as his head flew back. They started to really get into it as John and Sarah watched with confusion, then with smiles.

"C'mon, let's go down there," John grabbed Sarah's hand and pointed to another pool lower down. They hopped in, and John took off his clothes, then Sarah's. He pulled in her closer and started to kiss her on the neck. He moved his hands down to her lower back, and they made love right then and there while Charlie and Panther beat the crap out of each other.

In the woods were a few sets of curious eyes watching and wondering who in the world were these strangers fighting and having sex in their river. The men had bows slung over their shoulders, and kept their young sons safe behind them as they contemplated on what to do, if anything at all. The leader of the group decided to make himself seen to the strange mix of people. Panther, having held Charlie under water for a few seconds, was looking off into the trees, and saw the man first. He let him up and Charlie came up with a big smile, ready for more, but then he saw that his father was looking somewhere, quite intently. Charlie turned around and saw the man, as well as other faces poking out of the trees. Seeing that Panther was unarmed, the man was not threatened. Panther waved and smiled. The man nodded in acknowledgement. Charlie just looked in wonder at the man dressed only in a loin cloth, holding a large spear, and donning various beaded necklaces, bracelets, and large plugs in his ear lobes.

Panther stepped forward with a smile. The average-height, strong man stepped back and lifted his spear. Panther put his hands up, continued to smile and still moved forward.

"I am Panther of the Lakota Sioux," he said as he drew nearer to the man. "I am friend. Amigo. Yo soy amigo," he said not knowing what else to say, having picked up some Spanish. The man lowered his spear. "Nuestro un familia. Mi hijos. La chica es la novia de mi hijo. Nuestro amigos. No tienes miedo," Panther told him, in broken Spanish, hoping that he'd understand, that they were a family, that these were his sons, the girl was the girlfriend of his son, that they were friendly, and that he should not be afraid. At this point John and Sarah were listening to what was going on, and put their clothes back on, then walked up the bank to where Charlie and Panther were. The native man waved his people forward. Two men stood at either side of him, and the young boys poked their heads around.

"I have words of English," the man said, and then broke a smile to the group. Panther and his group smiled back. "You come, eat," the man said, as he stepped aside to display the wild pig they had just killed and was strapped to a pole. "Today is good."

"Oh wow, that's very kind of you! Thank you! Yes, yes, of course, c'mon guys," Panther said with a smile to his family, and they all followed, entranced by the moment.

They soon found themselves traveling an ancient path beat by centuries of natives. The natives moved quickly, and they had to move quickly to keep up. The young boys looked back with smiles at the strangers as they hurried along back to their village. The sun cascaded and beamed into openings of the canopy as a cool mountain breeze swept through the forest. Spirits were high, and the anticipation of entering into a world unknown tickled each of them. When they reached the village, the women were busy mashing corn, fires were lit, little kids ran around, babies were being nursed by their mothers in their little open shelters. Tiny pet monkeys jumped about, messing with the children, and everyone was happy. The hunting leader took the group directly to the elder, the leader of the clan, and introduced them. The man sat smoking a pipe, taking sips from a gourd. He had a long gray, braided pony tail, and time showed on his face. He had a frail looking body, and a wrinkled face. He looked up in acknowledgement of the people before him, and his eyes were very kind. His wife graciously got up from sitting inside of their home, and motioned the visitors to sit. She offered tea, and everyone most thankfully accepted, as they sat on the long grass covered floor.

"Friends," the hunting party leader said, and the old man smiled and nodded to the visitors.

"Thank you, this is very nice," John said with a smile as the sun shone into the entrance of the cozy shelter. "What is your name? "

"Nombre? I'm, John," John said as he pointed to himself. "John, I'm John. This is Sarah. That's Charlie. And he is Wes, or Panther. He is Panther," John said with a lot of nonverbal communication.

"Kicking Bird," he said and smiled. "Wife, Blue River."

"Oh, so you can speak English?" Charlie asked.

"No," he said with a big smile, and everyone laughed.

Night fell on the small village, and the feast, the celebration of life began. A large fire burned as the drums drove the vibration and tone for the night. Everyone ate, laughed, and lifted their heads high to the heavens, while their bodies connected to the earth and the ones that they loved. John, Charlie, Sarah, and Panther sat with full stomachs and smiles. A man soon came to them with three gourds, for each man.

"Drink, drink to see," he said and they all took the gourds without hesitation, not wanting to refuse their generosity. "You, you help," he said to Sarah. The guys eyed the drink, swirled it around and tried to get a look at it in the firelight.

"It's purple," John said as he half smiled. "Well, bottom's up."

"Wait, wait, hang on. This isn't any normal drink," Panther said. "If it's to see, then you will really see."

"I want to see, dad. I want to see."

"Yeah, me too," Charlie said.

"O.k., but just clear your mind, and have no fear," Panther said.

"What, you've drank this before?" Charlie asked with a little laugh.

"No, but something like it."

"O.k. Sarah, just keep an eye on us, o.k. baby?" John said as he leaned against her.

"What if I wanted to see too?" Sarah said with a smile.

"The man had a reason for asking you to look out for us. I'll tell you what I see, o.k.?"

"Aren't you scared?"

"No." John kissed Sarah, and then drank the drink along with his brother and father.

They sat for a half hour, feeling calm, and then the power of the mushroom tea hit them.

"The fire is dancing. I can see its dancers. I can see their faces. I can hear their voices. They're calling to me," Charlie said and then stood up in a trance. He walked slowly to the fire, drawn to it, then joined the dancing. His soul lifted, his mind lost to the power of the mushroom spirit. He danced in freedom. He danced with a joy that brought tears to his eyes. He looked to the starlit sky, spun with opened arms, and the tears wouldn't stop falling. He laughed in the waterfall of emotions that overcame him, as he wandered away from the fire. He left his body and was met by his mother in the starlit night. She took him by his hand as a child, and they ran through a field of yellow flowers.

"Dakota baby!" she exclaimed with joy as she lifted her baby boy into her arms and onto her chest.

"Momma! Why did you leave me?"

"I am here baby! I'll never leave you!"

"Yes, you did, you're going to leave me momma! Don't leave me momma!"

"Charlie! Charlie! It's o.k.," Sarah tried to stir Charlie from his state of mind as he laid in a patch of grass far from the fire, but was unable to.

"You left me, so did daddy! They hurt me, momma. They hurt me, momma!" Charlie said as he now floated in space, speaking as an adult with his child's heart, then his adult voice took over. All the while Sarah tried to stir him from his fetal position. She couldn't hear anything he was saying, only mumbling. She ran to John, but he was in a trance of his own . . . and the same for Panther. She went to the man who gave them the drinks.

"Are they o.k.?"

"Yes, just watch after, they are seeing," he said as he looked into the fire.

"I'm going to kill him. I will rip his heart out. The sicko raped a child! A small boy!" Charlie screamed with tears in his vision. He replayed the horror of his foster parent abusing him.

"His heart is already ripped from his body," Eagle's Claw said as he appeared to his great grandson. "He is doomed to the hell they preached of. Be at peace Charlie. What he tried to take has been restored to you by the Great Spirit."

"Who are you?" Charlie asked as he stood on a grassy plain, with the sun setting.

"I am your great grandfather. I hold your heart. I sit with your mother in the endless sky. You are Dakota. You are of a great nation. You are stronger than strength itself. Go to our people, open your arms to your father. He longs for you . . . ." Eagle's Claw disappeared.

"Wait, wait! Don't leave! I've killed men! I've killed men! It eats at my soul! I've killed men!" Eagle's Claw voice then spoke from the sky.

"It is the nature of war. I, too, have killed men. You saved your father. Cleanse and forgive yourself. It is your life to live without fear, guilt, or pain . . . it is your time to live as a strong Sioux man."

"How do I do this?" He screamed to the sky. Then a glow of warm, peaceful yellow glow fell over him, and he felt free. He fell to the plains. He heard the stomping feet of the buffalo, the chanting of his people, and then slowly woke up. The dancing of the Mexican natives continued as the fire burned late into the night. Charlie walked in a daze of firelight over to Sarah.

"Is Lakota o.k.? And my father, Panther?"

"They are in a dream state, Charlie. I don't know. They're both in and out of a sleep-like-state, just mumbling things. You guys shouldn't have drunk that stuff. It's scaring me, Charlie."

"Don't have fear. Our ancestors are speaking to us, they are comforting us. I am Dakota of the great Sioux nation . . . and you are my sister. Sit with me and tell me what's on your heart." Sarah was taken aback by Charlie, but could see peace in his eyes, like she had never seen before in them.

"O.k." Meanwhile John was lost in a dream. In his dream he was being tortured by all of the people who abused him in his life. They all stood around him laughing with devilish eyes. He lied on a cold concrete floor as they spit on him and taunted him, as tears flowed down his cheeks, forming a puddle. He screamed for them to stop, and that's when his vision turned. Suddenly, he found himself atop of his father's shoulders looking down at his momma and Dakota in her arms. The same yellow light glowed as they all walked through a field of wildflowers. A circle of ancestors started to dance and sing around them, encircling them with love. Lakota smiled, and then awoke to Sarah and Dakota.

"Dakota, my baby brother . . . I love you," he said as he sat up and hugged his fully grown brother. "Sarah, my heart. I love you so much," he said as tears flowed down his face and he embraced her, too.

"We love you too, Lakota," they both said and all shared tears.

"Is dad alright?" Lakota asked.

"Yeah, we're just waiting for him to wake up," Sarah said as she kissed John's tears away. Panther was also lost in a dream. Lost in the cabin he built with his own two hands. Lost in the cabin where his children were born. Lost in the cabin where he laughed and played. Lost in the cabin where he made love to his wife. Lost in the memory of perfect love. Flashes of them all together, then flashes of them being destroyed were going back and forth. Flashes of peace before. Flashes of hell after. Flashes of his wife dying on the floor. Flashes of him in the winter cold with his two boys, scared like never before. Flashes of prison. Flashes of war. Then always flashing back to them all together in the cabin. Voices calling to him, calling him back to his people. Voices calling him back to his land. Then he awoke, just like Charlie and John. He silently scooted over to them with tears in his eyes, and looked into the fire.

"I love you all," he said without moving his eyes from the fire. "Our people are calling."

"I know. I am Dakota of the great Sioux nation. I hear them too."

"I am Lakota, father. We must go home." Sarah just looked at all of them, and knew.

"I will follow," she said with a smile. "I will follow my new family to the ends of the earth."

Morning came to the now sleepy village, and it was stirred in all of their hearts to travel back into the land of their ancestors. Sarah was dedicated to them, as she was from the start, and also promised John that she would contact her parents as soon as possible. They thanked their friendly hosts, packed what little they had, and began their journey home. A journey that wasn't going to be easy, and was very uncertain. They were, after all, on the run from the law. Not only were they AWOL from the U.S. Navy, but they were fugitives for murder. They were, however, determined to make it back across the border, one way or another, and return to their people. A decision made not by mushroom-induced hallucinations, but by decisions made from the heart no matter the consequences. They traveled for a couple of months, and were back at the Mexican-American border.

"So, we all know the plan, and we just have to go for it . . . o.k.?" Panther said as he looked at the river before them. "We'll cross over there." They had no choice but to sneak back into the U.S. illegally, and so they did it where no one was watching by the cover of night that was soon turning to dawn. In no time at all, they were back on U.S. soil in Texas.

"So, now we just head north huh?" Dakota asked with a full beard and hair down past his shoulders, just like his brother and father.

"Yep," Panther said as he adjusted his pack.

"And then what?" Lakota wondered as he held Sarah's hand.

"We'll know when we get there," Panther responded with a smile. "Let's just focus on staying low profile . . . if that's at all possible. We look kind of rough, and I'm not so sure how friendly the people are around here to Native Americans."

"Well, there's no one around," Sarah said as she looked out onto the desert-like terrain. "But, I see what you mean . . . although a clean look would possibly blow your cover. I'm keeping my braid, native clothes, and tan skin. If they want to mess with us, then they'll be messing with the wrong guys," she said with a smile.

"If we only had some horses," Dakota said as the sun began to rise.

"Well, if you come across a few, you let me know," Panther said as he patted Dakota on the back.

"Oh, I'll be looking."

"Look out for rattlesnakes while you're at it," Lakota said and pretended to see one behind Dakota.

"Huh, what, oh pis!" Dakota jumped back and turned at the same time. "You prick!"

"Yes, I am Great Butthole, son of Panther, brother to Weinerface," Lakota said jokingly as they walked along, with gourds of river water knocking against their hips as they traveled. "Speaking of which, dad, shouldn't we have names like Panther?"

"Right, I mean you weren't born with that name, right?"

"No, it was given to me by my actions."

"O.k., so Dakota and I need to have these names too, as well as Sarah."

"Yes, in time. Once we reach our people, they will be glad to give you names."

Civilization was not too far ahead, and the first thing they came across heading north, was a train heading their direction. So, they hopped aboard a slow moving boxcar and went along for the ride. They stayed well hidden, eating the little food they brought along, and traveled for hundreds of miles without stopping but one time. They hid well when the conductor did a quick walkabout, and then it was non-stop to Oregon. They hopped off like scurrying roaches, hid in the woods until it was clear, and then regrouped.

"Now we head east. At least we have a bit of summer left . . . though the cold will be coming soon," Panther said. "We'll make it to the cabin very soon, especially if we can hop another train."

"Is that going to be safe, dad?" Lakota asked. "Won't we be better off at the reservation? We are returning to our people after all, right?"

"Yes, but, I have to see if it's still there," Panther said with great pain his eyes.

"O.k., dad."

"I just hope I find some hot Lakota girl . . . I'm dying here," Dakota said.

"You will," Sarah said as they kept walking.

"We need to eat something substantial. Don't you think, boys?" Panther said as he looked around for a suitable stick. "I hear water up ahead. How about some fish for dinner?"

"Sounds good to me," Lakota answered and started looking for strong saplings right at the same time Sarah and Dakota did too.

"Remember that fat 'ol fish I speared on the coast? That was crazy! I don't know what I was thinking . . ." Dakota said.

"You weren't, you dumbass," Lakota said with a smile. "You should've been eaten alive when that shark got a whiff of your fish."

"No shark can take me. I'm one with sharks. Hey, that's it! That's my name! One With Sharks! Right, huh?"

"Maybe, Dakota, maybe. The thing is, you don't name yourself. Otherwise people would have names like "Big Penis" or "Hung Like Horse" . . . do you see what I'm saying?" Panther said.

"Yes!" Dakota was so happy but his laughter was cut short by a burning need to ask his father a question. "How did you get your name anyways, dad?"

"I went on a vision quest," he simply replied.

"That's it?" Dakota asked with a look of confusion as Lakota and Sarah listened intently.

"Well, that's what we do. When I was thirteen, I was sent out, by my father, alone for about five days to fast and connect to nature and the Great Spirit. On the fourth day, after starting to really lose hope, I was overwhelmed with great comfort and peace. And I went into a trance-like state. I can remember like it was yesterday. In my vision, I was lost in the wilderness and I started to panic. But, my fear was cut short by a beautiful jet black Panther. It approached me and stared into my soul with its striking green eyes. I stood in disbelief as it walked right up to me and rubbed its head against my chest. He slowly walked ahead of me into a sun drenched meadow and I followed," Panther explained with a smile in his eyes. They all looked at him with a shared smile and greater understanding.

"Well, that's a pretty good name. I'll work on a new one for you . . . now that you're older . . . something more fitting," Dakota said with a smile and a pat on the back for his dad.

"What was your father's name?" Lakota asked.

"Whispers of the Wind," Panther said with a smile and then looked to the sky.

"How come you haven't talked about him, or your mother?" Lakota continued in curiosity.

"Well, I don't know really. I guess I came to peace with their death and they live with me in my heart ... so. But, I can tell you this. Your grandfather was an amazing man. He never gave in to the ways of the white man, nor did he live with hate. He made me the man I am today. He loved me very much. He loves you boys very much as well. You might not know it, but he watches over us. Same with your grandmother. She was an incredibly strong, loving woman. She would give anything to be here with us. Just as your mother would. Your mother loves you boys so ..." Panther was unable to talk, cut short by rising emotions and tears. He looked deeply into the eyes of his boys and new daughter. Lakota welled with tears, as did Sarah and Dakota. They all walked to Panther with open arms and collectively embraced him with their love.

"Say no more, Dad," Lakota said as he held his father.

They ate well that night, having speared a few fish in a pool off to the side of the river, and then slept well under the starry sky. Lakota and Sarah laid together, not far from the fire and talked quietly while Panther and Dakota slept.

"If I tell my parents the whole story, they might freak out . . . no, no, they will freak out."

"When will you ever see them again? How can we keep this up? You have to see them some time, right?"

"Don't you think our story's been all over the news? I think they know already. The last time I called them, my mom was desperate to see me, and I don't think they believed the Peace Corps thing. I mean c'mon, they're not stupid. I'm sure you were identified, and they knew I was coming out to see you. C'mon, John, we've been over this time and time again."

"Yeah, but what if the whole story is what they need to hear? Don't you want them to see our children?"

"Children?" Sarah rolled over and put her head on Lakota's chest.

"Yes, of course. I mean, let's just say you write them a letter, explaining everything . . . don't you think they'd understand? Or would they call the dogs on me?"

"I don't know. And how would I find out anything . . . we'd have to be settled somewhere for them to write back. Maybe I'll wait until we get to the reservation."

"I don't think we'll be staying there. My father's got something planned, but I have no idea what."

"Oh, John, I don't know. Do you want to know the truth?"

"Yeah, of course."

"My father . . . well, umm, my father was . . . is . . . a drunk. He's been abusive to my mom and me since forever. I feel bad for my mom, but I don't know what to tell her. She feels trapped or something, like my father would kill her if she left. . . ."

"Oh, I'm so sorry, baby."

"Yeah, well, I've waited my entire life for this moment right here. Freedom. And if my mom doesn't want to seek after it herself, then . . . well, I can't make her. But for once in my life I am alive. I am in love. And I am willing to do, and go, wherever, as long as it's with you," Sarah said as a tear dropped down her cheek, lit by the firelight. Lakota looked her deep into her eyes, wiped away the tear, and kissed her gently.

"Me, too." They made sweet, soft love under the starry sky and fell asleep in bliss.

Morning came and the family headed east, following Panther on his quest for a reconnection with his previous home—a reconnection with the emotions that he had buried deep away in his heart. They were all on a quest and all on the run.

"So, dad, when do you suppose we'll get there?" Lakota asked as he walked hand-in-hand with Sarah.

"When the scent of the wildflowers overpowers your senses, and the rush of knowing comes to your heart," he said as he walked swiftly ahead.

"That's really beautiful, dad, no really, but we need to hop that other train . . . don't you think? I mean, shoot, we don't want to freeze to death huh . . . by the time we get there and all," Dakota said straight forward.

"O.k." Panther said with his eyes fixed to the east.

"O.k., good."

They soon found a slow-moving train and hopped aboard. They rode east for the next few days, then hopped off only miles from their home. They were tired, hungry, and ready for a change.

"This is really beautiful country," Sarah said with a smile.

"Need rabbit. Need food," Dakota said as he eyed the grassland with hawk eyes.

"Good luck," Panther said with a smile as the sun began to sit around six o'clock, fall was upon them, casting a glow upon the prairie.

"You just watch old man," Dakota said as he pulled a sling shot from his back pocket.

"Where in the hell did you find that?" Lakota asked with a laugh for his determined brother.

"Just now, back in our luxury boxcar my friend. Now help me find a rock and shut up," he said as he eyed the rabbit.

"Right, sure, we'll get on that," Lakota smiled at Sarah and they all looked around for some rocks.

"Here, try this one," Panther said as they all crouched down. Dakota drew the sling back, took aim, and let the rock fly. It hit the rabbit directly in the chest and knocked it out.

"Yes!" Dakota ran up to the rabbit to claim his prize. He snatched it up by the hind legs and lifted it up proudly to the smiling crew. He started to walk and that's when the resurrection came. The rabbit sprang to life and startled the life out of poor Dakota. But his stomach was directly related to his grip, and the rabbit wasn't going anywhere. Dakota grabbed the hare by its throat and was choking the flailing beast, trying not to make eye contact. After a minute the kicking stopped and that's when the hysterical laughter set in for his awaiting family.

"You laugh now, but we'll see who's laughing when you guys are gnawing on grass. Shoot. This is my rabbit now!" Dakota said seriously holding the fat limp rabbit.

"Nice moves, little bro. You sure choked the crap out of it."

"Screw off," Dakota said and then looked away trying not to laugh. "You can have his colon . . . if you're lucky!" Dakota said now bursting into hysterical laughter.

"Yes! My favorite part!"

"Mine too! Rabbit ass!" Sarah exclaimed loudly with laughter tears falling down her face. That's when everyone went dead silent and looked at her with wondering eyes. "What?" Sarah said and wiped her face while continuing to laugh. That's when everyone fell to the ground in complete hysterics.

They moved on foot, trying to keep a low profile . . . they were, after all, wanted. So they moved as wanted people. When they found some cover in a stand of trees, they decided to camp for the night.

They lit a small fire, and feasted on rabbit.

"Dad, this isn't going to last you know," Lakota said.

"What, this rabbit?"

"No. Us. On the run. We've got to cross either border as soon as possible. I'm surprised we've made it this far. I'm not so sure that returning to the reservation is such a good idea."

"What? I thought it was the plan to return to our people . . . at least visit."

"I don't know. It's just a feelin' I got all of a sudden, like a lightning bolt to my head. I'm sure it's alright. Is the reservation a safe place . . . a separated sanctity of sorts?"

"Not exactly," Panther said as he wiped his mouth with his sleeve.

"So, let me get this straight. Correct me if I'm wrong. The first people we come across, our own people, will turn us in? I mean, I'm sure there are posters with rewards on our heads," Dakota said. "I think this reality is hitting me too. We're fugitives. Bro, you're right, I don't know what we've been thinking, or not been thinking of . . . but we're gonna be screwed if we're spotted. I mean look at us, three guys and a white girl. We're just begging to be caught." Dakota looked around the fire at all of their faces with a look of fear in his brown eyes lit up in the flames.

"Maybe they're right," Sarah said as she gripped Lakota's arm and put her head on his shoulder.

"We need to at least make it to the old house. We've come this far," Panther said with conviction. "I have to at least . . . . I could care less about the box, you know, the reservation, now the people there . . . well of course I care about them . . . but what can I do?"

"O.k., so why haven't we been talking about this the whole time? We've been in some kind of fantasy world or something. We can't live the old Sioux way. We can't just return to this place that I thought was safe or something. You should have smacked us out of this dad," Lakota said rather perturbed, both at himself and his father.

"Now hang on. We all made the decision together," Panther retorted.

"Yeah, well that tea wore off a long time ago, but the dream lingered, now I'm fearing a nightmare," Dakota said as he threw a rock into the fire. "Let's just go our separate ways. I'm clearly an odd man out. John, you and Sarah go together, run like the wind. And dad, well, I don't know. You obviously need closure from the old house, so, get it. I've tagged along long enough. I'm outta here first thing in the morning."

"Wait, wait, hang on," Lakota said. "There's gotta be a better way."

"Yeah, Dakota, don't leave," Sarah said with sincerity.

"I love you guys and all, but it's time for me to forge my own path. Dad, you get what you need and John, you and Sarah run. Go make babies in safety for God's sake. I don't know what we've been thinking. But, hey, it's been real."

"I got what I need, Dakota," Panther said.

"Let's just stick with the name Charlie dad. I'm not an Indian. I'm a kid from Kansas. And I'll be damned if I spend a minute in any prison. I just started to live when they called me up. I'm complete now. I know where I'm from; now I need to figure out where I'm going." Panther couldn't argue with his son, as his words seemed all too familiar.

"O.k. Charlie."

"Where you gonna go?" Lakota asked.

"Back south. What about you?"

"To the place I was born. To the place mom was taken from us. I need what dad needs, then we can go," Lakota said as he looked at Sarah and then his dad.

"Alright. Well, just promise me you'll make it quick," Dakota said.

"I don't know, Lakota. We should all go. This is a bad omen. We can travel together, to the south once again, then go our separate ways," Panther said with great concern, having heard all of the words spoken.

"O.k., we'll sleep on it," Lakota said with a pensive look in his eye and laid back on the ground. Sarah laid on his arm.

The fire burned down to a hot bed of orange glowing coals and sent off only a wisp of smoke as everyone deeply slept. Six hours passed.

"Rise and shine," a typical cowboy looking fellow said loudly with a three quarters moon at his back. His partner stood next to him, both with pointed rifles. Panther awoke first. The men poked the rest awake with their feet. "It ain't morning, and I ain't your momma with breakfast in bed."

John and Sarah woke up, sat up, and were frozen with fear as well as confusion. "Well, it's been a good run, but like they say, all good things must come to an end. You see, me and my partner here are bounty hunters, and well, consider your selves successfully hunted," he said with a smile, then spit tobacco juice from his mouth onto the glowing coals.

When the man pointed his rifle at Sarah, John put himself in front of her. "Oh, I got it, well that's just fine." He walked towards her with his gun pointed directly at her head. He dug the barrel into her temple. "That's the great thing about a rifle. The guy who's got it has all the power. I hadn't seen such a pretty fugitive ever."

"Hey, c'mon, you don't want to go there," John said as he looked the man in the eye.

"That's funny, no really, that's good. You're gonna love watching me violate your little girly here. I guarantee it." John's blood boiled as the man forced Sarah on to her back with his gun. The man's partner kept everyone under gun point, pointing the rifle back and forth to each man.

"Hey, shouldn't we tie these guys up first?" his partner said clearly concerned about the three-to-one odds.

Just as the cowboy moved his gun away from Sarah, Lakota grabbed the gun and the two men struggled for possession and control of the rifle. "Shoot the bastard!" the cowboy yelled.

"They ain't any good to us dead!" the sidekick yelled in a panic as he yelled for the other men to keep their hands up and frantically pointed the gun between Dakota and Panther. And then, BAM! The rifle went off and the bullet found the worst possible landing place . . . Dakota. Dakota fell over in a pool of blood. Everyone momentarily froze. The cowboy ripped the gun away from Lakota's stunned, limp hands, cocked the rifle and pointed it at him. Panther stared at his fallen son, and then in a fury of rage charged the cowboy, only to be stopped short by a bullet to his head straight from the barrel of the bounty hunter who had previously been frantically waving his rifle. Both bounty hunters rushed with both rifles pointed at John and Sarah. Sarah was hysterical in tears, and John was frozen, caught in a slow motion nightmare.

"Damn it! You see what you made us go and do! Huh! What!" the cowboy yelled and then knocked a stunned John out with a mighty blow to the head with the butt of his gun.

"So, what do we do?"

"We shut this whore up. Gag her. Tie her hands together, then do the same with Mr. Hero here. Dumb ass got his partners killed. Stupid bastard."

The bounty hunters left Panther and Dakota for dead and dragged off Lakota and Sarah.

8

DAKOTA LEFT HIS BLEEDING BODY WITH A BULLET HOLE THAT WENT clear through his side and out the other.

"No, Dakota, you're not ready yet," his mom said to him in spirit.

"Why not, this is nice. This is really nice mom . . . I mean, why . . . what do . . . I can't . . . ," Dakota said as his eyes started to tear.

"Yes you can," she said with peaceful power. And with that Dakota's eyes opened. The sun was bright, as he opened his eyes and tried to adjust them. The pain was excruciating. His father was draped over him, his hand resting on Dakota's face that was dug into the ground. He managed to roll his father's body off exposing his face. When he looked down he wanted to die at the sight. His emotions were locked, his body in a state of shock, and that's when he looked down at his own non-fatal wounds. It was steadily bleeding, and he could barely move. But he had to. He looked over to his father as he dragged himself into a patch of grass in the shade. His father's knife caught the sun and sparkled. Dakota crawled over to the knife, and took it from his father's side. He kissed his father's cheek as a tear rolled down his face and then made his way to the nearly dead coals of the fire from the night before. He painstakingly pulled some twigs together and stoked the fire once again. The fire rose up and Charlie put the knife to the flame and cooked it until it was red hot. He lifted his shirt, put a handful of the shirt into his mouth, and then cauterized the front wound as blood slowly poured out.

"Ahhhhhhhhh! Oh my . . . !" he muffled his scream so as to not bring attention. He knew that it wouldn't be long before they would be coming for their bodies. Then Dakota started the process all over and put the red hot knife to his back flank. The pain was like nothing he had ever experienced. He drank water from one of their gourds, gathered up some scraps from the rabbit, strapped the gourd and knife to his body, covered his father with a blanket and crawled off into the woods.

John and Sarah were being dragged behind two horses. They were now prisoners, being pulled along by their wrists at a fast trot. The sun beat down as they crossed the plains towards a small city where they were to be turned over for a hefty ransom.

"I'm telling you, man, look at this picture. We lucked out. This is the murderer himself," the cowboy said as he handed his partner a piece of paper. "Regular war hero. Ain't that right Petty Officer John Rosenthal? And your little girl friend, Sarah J. Smith?"

"I am Lakota of the great Sioux nation. You killed my father and brother. You are my sworn enemy and I hope there's room in hell for you," John said in a muffle, with strength behind tears.

"Oh yeah, you don't say! All's I know is that you are lookin' at life in prison, your girl something quite awful, and me and my partner here are going to have saddle bags full of money . . . so, I don't care what your trying to say, and your daddy and brother for damned sure asked for it . . . if that's what your all worked up about. So you two just shut up, and we'll get you into the right hands so as to get you a nice, civil, fair trial . . . ," he said and then started to laugh. "Let's smoke to that. What do you say, partner!" He pulled out a couple of hand rolled cigarettes, passed one to his partner and they smoked. John looked at Sarah and their eyes spoke a thousand words as endless tears fell while they ran, trying to keep pace with the horses.

They soon reached a small town and were turned over to the local sheriff. After being identified they were locked in separate cells. The bounty hunters were questioned, they recounted the attack and their self-defense shooting of the other two in the party and then they were paid in full. Then, just as soon as they arrived, they left.

"John!" Sarah yelled from her cold, damp, foul smelling cell. "John!"

"It's o.k., it's o.k.!" John tried to console her without sight from ten cells away.

"Shut the hell up you whiny bitches!" a random man yelled from his cell.

"You shut the hell up! I'll rip your heart out, you scum!" John screamed as he clenched the bars. He turned red, veins popped from his forehead as he tried in vain to bend the bars. "AHHH!" It was then that John's cell was opened by a guard, who was backed by another.

"Now, just calm down there young man," the man said and then delivered a blow to Lakota's face with the butt of his gun. "Say another word, and we'll cut out your tongue. Hear me? Good. And don't you worry, you'll only be here for a few days before you get to your permanent home. Just so happens, you killed the son-in-law of a very important man in Washington D.C."

"What?" John said as he wiped blood from his shirt.

"Oh, you didn't know? Oh, now that's good! Yeah, that's real good. You're gonna fry . . . oh yeah, fry!"

"Oh my God, oh my God . . . ," John hung his head and tried to hide his tears.

"Yeah, yeah, it's o.k. I'd be crying too," the guard said and then rolled the cell door back with a loud slam.

A month later, John and Sarah were sitting in a court, both shackled at the wrists and ankles. They had been imprisoned in two separate facilities. Sarah at the State Women's Correctional Facility and John at San Quentin State Penitentiary. They were assigned a public defender and sat in front of the judge. John for murder and Sarah for aiding and abetting a criminal. Sarah's mother sat in the crowd, helpless and in a state of disbelief. Since the crime heavily involved a civilian, the Military turned the case over to the general court system. Nonetheless, all the players were there.

"All rise," the bailiff said as the rather annoyed-looking judge entered the court room. "Honorable Judge Dodson." The judge climbed the wooden stairs and sat at his mahogany throne of judgment.

"O.k., o.k.," he said as he gave a loud knock from his gavel. "Let's not make this any longer than it has to be. John sat along with everyone else and the surreal, numbing process began. "Petty Officer John Rosenthal you are on trial for the murder of Officer Martin Lewis, and Sarah Smith for aiding and abetting the criminal. Defense, how do you plea for the charge of murder in the first degree?" John's Lawyer stood and plead not-guilty. "Fine, then. Prosecution, your opening statement."

"Yes, your honor." The sharp dressed, handsome Prosecuting Attorney walked slowly with his hands in his pockets and addressed the hand-picked jury by both the prosecution and defense. He faced the jury from close range and made serious, yet comfortable, trusting eye contact as he spoke. "You will see without a shadow of a doubt that this was a situation fueled by anger, jealousy, and rage . . . not the defense of a woman or defense of an innocent brother as they will try to persuade you to believe, but rather a fight that was started by John Rosenthal and ended by John Rosenthal in cold-blooded murder. Do not be swayed by emotions, for it is solely facts that matter here today. And the FACT is John Rosenthal stabbed and killed an innocent man, Martin Lewis. That is all."

"Defense, your opening statement please."

"Yes, your honor." John and Sarah's older, seasoned attorney stood and approached the jury. "Good morning ladies and gentlemen. Thank you for serving the state of California by being here today. There is no doubt that my client killed a man, but the doubt is that he did this in cold blood, but rather in reaction and defense. John Rosenthal merely reacted to his soon to be fiance's impending rape, and his brother's impending murder. Now, I don't know about you, but I would be inclined to do the same. All I would ask of you is to search your hearts, because contrary to the prosecutions' stance, this is all about emotion . . . and this emotion is love. Acting out of love is not a crime, and we will prove without a shadow of a doubt that both Officer Robertson and Officer Lewis acted out of malice, aforethought when they dragged Sarah Smith into the alley to rape her. That is all."

"Is there any admitable evidence from either side, besides the photos I have here from the crime scene?" the judge asked as he looked down and out as to see past his spectacles.

"No, your honor," the prosecution replied as well as the defense. "I would like to call to the stand our first witness, if it pleases the court. Oh and if I may, I would like the jury to see the photos of the crime scene first and foremost."

"Yes, fine," the judge nodded. The jury was able to see the very raw, bloody pictures of the dead body laid upon the ground. Their faces told the entire story as each picture was passed from one juror to the next. John hung his head, reliving every last second of the scene. The prosecution then called to the stand the man who arrived on the scene first, a bouncer from the club. "I would like to call to the stand Mr. Mike Castanza." Mr. Castanza approached the stand, was sworn in, and then had a seat. "Now, Mr. Castanza can you describe what you saw that night?"

"Yes sir. Someone from the club approached me as to a possible disturbance going on outside of the side door and so naturally I checked it out. The first thing that I saw was a dead body . . . blood everywhere. I almost fainted from the sight of it, ya know?"

"Right, o.k., go on."

"Well, just as soon as I turned to run back in for help, I heard a muffled yelling from behind a dumpster. My heart was racing, but I knew that I had to check it out . . . so I did. That's when I found Officer Robertson tied up and gagged. I used my pocket knife to untie him and pulled out his gag. He was really worked up, really angry, and told me what happened right then and there."

"O.k., what did he say?"

"Well, he said that he and his buddy had met two single girls. He said the one girl was about to come out, and so Officer Robertson was foolin' around with Sarah until her friend showed up. That's when he told me that a group of three men came running from the front of the club, down the alley and attacked them. He said that he was beat up by one man, all of the men were in uniform he said, and the others teamed up on Officer Lewis. He said that the one guy had his buddy pinned, and the next thing he knew was that his friend was stabbed and killed. Then they knocked him out. I was terrified, ya know, and so I ran into the club with Officer Robertson and we called the police."

"Is that all?"

"Yes, sir, that's all."

"O.k., that's fine, sir. Defense, your witness." John's lawyer stood up and approached the witness with confidence, then spoke.

"Now you know, sir, that this is just the story of a rapist? Don't you?" he said as he looked deep into the eyes of the nervous bouncer.

"Objection your honor," prosecution stood and plead his objection.

"Sustained," the judge said.

"Right, fine. Now you appear to be a smart man, Mr. Castanza. Is that fair to say?"

"Well, I guess you could say that."

"Do you have a high school or college degree?"

"Objection! This man's educational background is not on trial!"

"Sustained. Please, get to your point, and question the man fairly," the judge said as he sat back in his chair.

"The point I'm trying to make here is simple. This man's testimony should be taken with a grain of salt, as he himself would agree to this question . . . do you believe this is just one man's side of the story and not the complete truth or even part of the truth?"

"Yes, I mean, it's just what I was told by Officer Robertson. That is all."

"Exactly, that is all. No further questions your honor. Thank you, Mr. Castanza."

"Any further questioning?" the judge asked and both sides said no. "Does the defense have a witness they would like to call?"

"Yes, your honor, Ralph James." Ralph James was the bar tender working the night of the murder and was happy to testify to what he saw and heard that night. He was sworn in and then John's attorney began questioning him. "So, Mr. James, you were working the night of the murder, is this correct?"

"Yes, sir."

"Now, I have here the official police report that tells of Officer Robertson's story. It says, just like Mr. Castanza recounts, that Sarah Smith was with a friend that night. Is this true?"

"No." The jury made some noise and stirred a bit. "She was alone and appeared to be waiting for someone."

"Now, did you see John Rosenthal that evening?"

"Yes, he was with two other men, and very concerned for the safety and whereabouts of a woman he was supposed to meet."

"So, would you say he was looking for her and she was waiting for him?"

"Yes, I mean . . ."

"Objection, leading the witness."

"Overruled. Continue Mr. James."

"I mean yes, it appeared to be that way."

"Did you see Officer Robertson or Officer Lewis bothering her at all during the course of her wait?"

"I saw plenty of guys trying to get her attention, so I couldn't say whether or not any of the men were the men you speak of."

"Did you see this man, Officer Robertson, talking to her at any point in the evening?"

"I can't say for sure."

"Was she inviting to any of the men?"

"No, most certainly not. I mean she was the prettiest girl in the joint that night, so she was getting a lot of attention, but no, she was not smiling nor inviting nor talking to anyone."

"Did you ever see her with another woman, like a friend, or sister?"

"No."

"Thank you, no further questions." The prosecution stood up and cross-examined the witness.

"Could you, without a shadow of a doubt, say that she was waiting for a man as opposed to a friend or sister?"

"No."

"So you're saying that she could have been waiting for anyone, or at least appeared to be waiting for someone, is this correct?"

"Yes, but after working a bar for such a long time, you start to get a feel for things. You know people. She appeared to be waiting for a date, and this was solidified in my mind when the man came looking for her."

"But, you couldn't say, at the time, what the situation was exactly, is that correct?"

"Correct."

"Thank you, no further questions your honor."

"If I may, your honor, I'd like to call Officer Robertson to the stand," the defense attorney, Roger Shumacker, calmly said from his seat while John and Sarah both stirred.

"You may." The Officer was sworn in and took the stand. John's lawyer strolled up to the witness stand.

"Officer Robertson, is it true that you were waiting for your friend, Officer Lewis' girl to join you and Sarah Smith that evening in the alley?"

"Yes, sir."

"Well, I must be mistaken. I thought it was Sarah Smith's friend, not Officer Lewis' girl, which by the way Officer Lewis was a married man, with children. What would he be doing with a date? Or even some girl he just met?"

"Well, I mean, I'm not his mother. He knew what he was doing."

"So was he there with a date, or did he just meet Sarah's imaginary friend that night, as your confession states?"

"It was Sarah's friend. That's it."

"Did you know that Sarah was there that evening because her boyfriend, John Rosenthal was going to meet her there?"

"Yes, sir. She was very unsure about their relationship and was willing to take a walk with me. She was distraught. So, the girl she was talking with near the pay phones, agreed to come with. So, I got Officer Lewis, and we went back to Sarah. Sarah said that her friend was going to be a minute in the ladies' room, so we all just went outside."

"Into the alley, where no one could see you?"

"Well, yeah, it's not that uncommon."

"So, it didn't take very long for you to persuade Sarah to kiss you and such, is this correct? I mean, how long could the girl have been in the bathroom?"

"I don't know, you know broads. And yeah, what can I say, I'm a lady's man," he said with a cocky little snicker.

"And Officer Lewis just stood watching?"

"I guess."

"Or was he there to stand watch and waiting for his turn to rape Sarah Smith?"

"Objection! Badgering the witness!" The prosecuting attorney jumped to his feet.

"Overruled."

"The truth is, you coerced, more than likely by force, with your buddy, Sarah Smith into the alley to rape her, and then your buddy was going to take his adulterous turn next if it wouldn't have been for the rushing men. Am I right?"

"No! No! What?! Screw you!" Officer Robertson slammed his fist and jumped to his feet. The jury was shocked and wide eyed, some frightened.

"Order! Order!" the judge smacked his gavel loudly. "Officer Robertson, you will act civilly or will be held in contempt of court. Carry on."

"I have no further questions, your honor." The prosecuting attorney approached the stand.

"Officer Robertson you and Officer Lewis were good friends, is this correct?"

"Pretty good friends. I mean he wasn't my best friend, but he was a nice guy and fun to hang out with."

"Right, o.k. Now, in your opinion do you think that he had any intention of cheating on his wife with either of the girls?"

"No, sir. He wasn't afraid to flirt a little, but he had no intention of cheating on his wife."

"O.k. Now, when you were rushed who attacked you?"

"John Rosenthal's father."

"And he did what?"

"He caught me by surprise and knocked me to the ground. We fought, and at the same time Officer Lewis was in a fight with Rosenthal's brother. Next thing I know Rosenthal is over the back of Officer Lewis looking stunned with a bloody knife in his hand. Martin died right then and there. They knocked me out, tied me up, ran off, and that's it. I was found by the bouncer, and that's it."

"So, all you know is that you were kissing an unmarried woman when you were brutally attacked and then your good friend was stabbed to death, is that correct?"

"Yeah. That's it."

"No further questions, your honor."

"You may step down if there are no further questions."

"Thank you, your honor," Robertson said as a bead of sweat fell off his forehead and onto his shoe. "My client Sarah Smith would like to testify your honor, if it pleases the court."

"Yes, bailiff escort Mrs. Smith to the stand." Sarah was sworn in and the questioning began by her own attorney.

"So, Sarah, why don't you just tell us what happened that night. O.k.?"

"O.k., I'd be glad to. My one and only love, for whom I had no doubt about our love, was returning home on leave from the islands. I flew out to San Diego to see him, and we planned on a meeting place for that evening. I told him beforehand that I would be wearing a red dress and a hat so that he would have no trouble finding me. I was alone, no friends, no sisters, nobody, just me. I was beyond excited to see him and as time passed I began to worry."

"How much time passed before you started to worry?"

"About a half hour. It wasn't like John to be late . . . ever. So, I left the table and went to the payphones. That's where I first saw Mr. Robertson and Mr. Lewis. I picked up the phone, put in some change, and began to dial John. There was no answer. I hung up the phone and that's when Mr. Robertson approached me in uniform. He asked me in a very gentlemanly manner if I was alright or not. I told him I was waiting for my boyfriend and told him John's name. He said that he knew John, which I know now was a lie, and he told me that sometimes military men get held up at the front of the club with technicalities like R&R passes. So, he and his friend convinced me in a very polite way to go with them, a back way if you will, so as to get John, his brother, and his father. I followed them out of the side door, which I never should have done, but I was a country girl, still am, and just trusted that these two polite gentlemen in uniform were going to help me. When the door slammed behind us, and I saw that we were in a dark alley I knew that I had made the wrong decision. I turned back quickly to open the door, but it self-locked and that's when Mr. Robertson forced me against the wall. He . . . he . . ."

"It's o.k., take your time."

"He pinned my hands against the wall and started to grope me, and reached up my dress. He pulled down my undergarments while Mr. Lewis just stood there laughing. I was screaming the entire time. That's when my family arrived. The rest happened rather quickly. John was wounded and so he was last on the scene. John's brother tackled Mr. Lewis from behind, John's father tackled Mr. Robertson and John protected me by positioning himself in front of me while the fights went on. The next thing I know John pulled his boot knife, and I looked to see why. Mr. Lewis had John's brother, Charlie, pinned and was about to stab him. John acted in defense just in the nick of time as Mr. Lewis was about to plunge his knife into Charlie. John stabbed Mr. Lewis in the back of the neck, and Mr. Lewis fell over dead. John was in complete shock. That's when John's dad knocked out Mr. Robertson with a final blow to the head. We all agreed that running was the only option. So they tied Mr. Robertson up. John was extremely hesitant to run. He didn't want to involve us, but we were all in it together. We knew that he wouldn't get a fair trial because he is a Native American and he killed a white senior officer. And so we ran to Mexico. All of us."

"Right, of course, I completely understand and appreciate your honesty. Now, looking back, do you regret the decision to run?"

"No, but yes. If we wouldn't have returned we could have lived in relative peace, but now we have lost two extremely important people in our lives, and I fear the most important person in my life is going to be lost to me because he reacted as any man would for their brother."

"I understand. It just doesn't seem fair now does it?"

"No, sir, it doesn't."

"Two men try to rape you, three men save you, one man tries to kill your future brother-in-law, and as a result is killed for his attempted act. AND on top of that you and John have lost the most important people in your lives due to the sickness of two men. AND due to the sickness of these two men, John is standing trial for murder and you for standing by your man. Is this correct?"

"Yes, sir. This is correct."

"No further questions your honor."

"Prosecution, . . ." the judge said as he lifted his eyebrows.

"Right, o.k. Now Mrs. Smith, let's just say for argument sake that you're telling the truth. Does it even matter?"

"Well, I sure hope so."

"We can go round and round as to who is telling the truth and who isn't, but that's not going to change the fact that John Rosenthal murdered a man and you ran with him to Mexico. Is this correct?"

"Well, I guess. But it does matter. The truth does matter. John acted out of love, and I acted out of love . . . and this most certainly matters."

"Well, that's all well and good, but that's not going to change the fact that John Rosenthal stabbed a man in the back of the neck, severing his spinal cord and killing him on the spot. Why not just kick the knife away from Mr. Lewis? Why murder?"

"He was shot in the leg sir, kicking wasn't an option."

"O.k., fair enough, but the fact is a man was murdered, and John is a murderer. Is this correct?"

"Yes, a man is dead, but no my John is not a murderer. He's a loving, strong, compassionate, protective man and he doesn't deserve this. He's a war hero, not a criminal."

"You truly love your man, don't you?"

"Yes, sir."

"Well, I'm sorry but love can't reverse murder, now can it? No further questions."

Sarah was escorted back to her chair and gave a loving glance to John.

"Are there any other testimonies that need to be heard?" the judge asked.

"My client John Rosenthal would like to address the court without examination, if it pleases the court."

"Go ahead." John cleared his throat and addressed the jury.

"Life is a tragic rollercoaster, and I have seen my ups and downs. I grew up an orphan, then was accepted into a loving home. I went off to college on a scholarship, and then was called to war. I've seen things and done things that no man should ever have to do—in the service of this country. A country that once belonged to a different race of people, my people. But I see humanity in all walks of life, and when I look at a man I don't look at color, but rather his actions. When my time in the islands ended, and I had made peace with my long lost brother and father, I felt on top of the world. I had a woman who loved me, and a country who embraced me. Not as an Indian, but as an American. After I acted out of defense to save the life of my brother, I felt the lowest of the low. Just a poor, orphaned Indian. So, we ran. There's not going to be a day that will go by that I won't wish that I hadn't run. So, yes, I acted out of love, but that doesn't change the fact that I killed a man. When I killed in war to protect our country I was given a medal, and when I killed in the real world to protect my brother I was given a different kind of metal. Metal bars and metal shackles on my wrists and ankles. This case is open and closed. I killed a man in defense. The love of my life followed me in support. She is innocent. That is all." John hung his head and was completely spent. He put his hands onto the desk and discretely grabbed a paper clip.

"O.k., alright, would the prosecution like to conclude?"

"No, your honor, we believe all has been said and heard."

"Prosecution?"

"No, no, we rest our case."

"Alright then. Jury you may deliberate, and we will meet back in a half hour for the final verdict."

The half hour seemed to be hours, but then the jury came out as the awaiting court sat in anticipation. The jury foreman stood and spoke on behalf of the jury.

"We the jury find the defendant John Rosenthal guilty of murder in the first degree, and we find Sarah Smith guilty of aiding and abetting."

"Fine. I hereby sentence John Rosenthal to a life sentence without parole in the control of San Quentin State Penitentiary. Sarah Smith, you will serve no less than two years of house arrest in lieu of incarceration. Case closed. Court adjourned. Bailiff escort Mr. Rosenthal if you would."

"No! John! You can't leave me!" Sarah screamed out and desperately tried to latch on to John. Her tears soaked his face as she kissed him one last time. John's heart melted then froze. A numbness like he had never experienced came over him, as the bailiff tore him from Sarah. "No! Lakota! Don't leave me! I'm pregnant John! You can't leave me! I'm having our baby! You see what you did? You bastard!" She screamed directly at Officer Robertson, then gave John a look of complete despair behind her red tearing eyes.

"What?!" John turned back and tried to get loose from the bailiff but another quickly assisted in securing him. "No! Sarah! A baby? Our baby!" John yelled out in tears. He was instantly ushered out of the court room. Both sets of adopted parents were devastated, as they sat in shock. Sarah's mom tried to console John's adopted mother as she wept, while Sarah's father sat indifferent.

Lakota sat shackled in the transport truck, along with about ten other men and two armed guards. His heart was being tormented as his mind flashed dozens of places at once. It was overwhelming him to the point of a near panic attack. It was then that a sudden calm came over him when his mom, dad, and brother appeared to him in his mind's eye.

"Calm your spirit, Lakota. Now's the time. We will see you through," Panther said as he appeared to his son in spirit, adorned in full Lakota garb. "Your unborn son is waiting, go now." John looked around and analyzed the situation. He was sitting alone in the very back seat, with no one across the aisle or next to him. He slipped out the paperclip, opened part of it and started working on his wrist cuffs. The military training for this very situation paid off as he nonchalantly looked around and out the windows in a calm manner and freed his wrist cuffs. He left them loose around his wrists in case a guard came and checked him out. He then slowly lifted his feet up to the seat and in a matter of thirty seconds he picked the lock on his ankle shackles. He slowly put his freed feet down, and then thought of what was next. They were only twenty minutes away from the prison and were in a stretch of open land. The guards stood watch, facing the prisoners. The driver, surprisingly, was exposed, without a cage between him and the prisoners, and so John came up with the only plan he could think of doing. He started coughing uncontrollably, making gagging noises and gasping for air. All of the prisoners turned back as he carried on.

"Go check it out will ya'," the one guard said to the other. John completely freed his shackles, but allowed the connecting chain from his feet to his hands look intact as he hunched over towards the window. The guard swiftly walked to the back of the truck and saw Lakota with his face smashed against the truck wall just beneath the window.

"Hey, hey," the guard poked Lakota with his left hand while keeping his shotgun pointed at him with his right. "Stop messin' around," the guard said and in a lightning flash Lakota turned in one swift motion, pinned the shotgun against the back of the seat, sprang up, and delivered a devastating blow to the guard's jaw. The guard flew back in agony and pulled the trigger, blasting a hole in the wall of the truck. Lakota pulled the shotgun away from the guard and then pulled the guard in by the leg so as to strike him with the butt end of the shotgun while maintaining cover. He struck the man's forehead with great force and knocked him out. He saw that it was a double barrel, and knew what he had to do next. The other guard came rushing with his shotgun lifted. John listened to the steps as if it were in a dream, and then at the perfect moment he popped out in a prone position and blasted the rushing guard's kneecaps out from under him. Lakota ran like a great Sioux warrior, grabbed his shotgun, and now had two shots remaining in the fully loaded gun. He then ran back to the other guard and shackled him at gun point. The truck was going crazy, men were trying to get out, rolling, crawling, yelling—it was chaos. Lakota knew he had to secure the next guard, and so he did. In a flash he ripped off his shirt and hog tied the guard. The driver was next.

"You already radioed backup, didn't you?" Lakota asked as he pointed the shotgun at the man's head.

"Yes, I did. Please, don't kill me."

"There won't be any need for that, you just do as I say, o.k.? That goes for all of you! Don't anyone move!" And with that Lakota looked out the front window, saw that they were on a straight away and then delivered a knockout blow to the driver. He quickly took the wheel, pulled the man from his seat and assumed the driver's position. He knew the driver would soon awake, so he quickly found a place to pull over. It was a small dirt road just off the main road that headed back into some trees. He only went so far, so the oncoming police nor onlooker could see the truck, but no so far so that the truck couldn't be found and the prisoners could be taken to prison. He quickly stripped the driver of his clothes, checking his pockets, took money from his wallet, took off his own clothes, all the while keeping the inmates at bay with verbal commands, and then put the drivers' clothes on himself. Then, he simply took the keys off one of the guards and eventually found the right one, after about five tries, then he let himself out of the truck, then locked the others in.

It was then that Lakota ran like he had never ran before, right back in the direction they had come from. His mind was fixated on one thought alone, and one voice. He was going to be a dad. Sarah's scream echoed throughout his entire being as he ran the race of his life.

"C'mon John!" Charlie's voice popped into John's mind as the freshman kid from Kansas. "Don't let them catch us! Faster! I'll race you to the top of that hill!" Lakota's mind and body believed the voice and could see Charlie in his imagination. A surge of energy came into Lakota, and he charged up the hill, zigzagging, losing his tracks through streams, hopping over logs, running for his life. He could hear tribal drums beating and beating. An overwhelming power came over him, as he nearly flew through the forest. He knew he had to head back north, off the peninsula, and into San Francisco where he could disappear then go after Sarah.

"Let our love fuel you and come home to me." Sarah's powerful words from her letter to John before the war was all Lakota thought as he ran full out without stopping. He stayed as hidden as possible as he ran, even if it was at points of speed crawling through low brush. He could hear the sirens, faint sounds of tracking dogs barking, and the sounds of searching planes. His senses were heightened like never before and scared like never before. A whole new sense of awareness, fear, and uncertainty coupled by an intense love was enveloping him now that he knew he was a father.

The land started to open up, more than he liked, and he was completely exposed as he entered into a more urban sprawl. It had been hours since he'd been running, and if he ran now then he'd look suspicious. So, his plan was to make it into the city as quickly as possible without attracting any attention. But he stuck out like a sore thumb . . . a wanted fugitive dressed as a guard. He had to act quickly. He could see road blocks in the distance, off to the right, and he could see the mighty Pacific off to the left. The choice was easy. Rocky coast, caves, and a whole lot of swimming. He made his way down the hill and was soon at the water. There was no one around, and like a chameleon he slowly made his way to the rocky coast.

The capture of Lakota was simple in the minds of the police. He was on a peninsula, and there was only one way out, to the north. So, low flying search planes were assigned to the beaches, as well as some boats, others still to zig zag formations across the land, and then road blocks were in place on all roads leading off of the peninsula. Dogs and search parties scoured the land, and it was a fairly simple recovery plan that was bound to work. But they underestimated the power of Lakota.

Lakota managed to make his way down to the frigid water undetected. The beach was nothing like he'd ever been on, nor the icy water. Jagged slippery rocks with pounding surf were his welcome, but he had no other option. He waited for a lull in the surf and then slid into the water like a seal and swam directly out to sea underwater for about a minute without taking a single breath, even though he felt like hyperventilating due to the shock of the fifty-degree water. When he did surface he only did for a second just allowing his mouth and nose to surface, then he went back down with his lungs full of air. He did this until he was completely free of the crushing surf, and then swam with all of his might, underwater, parallel to the beach. He didn't allow himself to slow down even though he started to feel pins and needles in his skin from the extremely cold water. He knew that if he could swim like this for the next half –hour that he would be well beyond the peninsula and out of the search radius. The beating of the drums got quieter in his mind, and soon it was complete silence. A strange warmth came over him and he swam, and he swam like a possessed creature, but his mind was starting to shut down. Lakota knew he could take no more, even though his body was on auto pilot as he surfaced like a scared arctic seal for the last time. He had to make one last push, or he would die of hypothermia in a matter of minutes. So, he did. And after being pounded by a few choice waves, and being crushed against a couple of jagged rocks, he pulled himself up out of the water onto the rocky coast. He was shaking and shivering as he frantically tried to find a place to hide. His thought process was slow, and he stumbled in search of some sort of place to conceal himself. He spotted a rocky overhang to which he was able to maneuver himself to, and then quickly took off his clothes. The sun warmed his frigid body as he sat naked on a sun-warmed rock. The rock felt so good that he draped himself over it, and his temperature slowly started to rise. He reached for his prison guard uniform and laid it out as well. The sun was low in the sky and lit his little nook just perfectly, a true gift from the Great Creator. He rested there and almost didn't feel like moving . . . ever. But he knew he had to, and that's all he wanted to do, when the time was right. He laid there looking out at the beautiful water, and thanked God he was alive. But he never felt so alone, because he was alone. He hadn't felt this way since he was just a boy, but now the loneliness was coupled by a hurt so deep that he couldn't even grasp it. He watched the sun and the tears just fell. What he had wanted his whole life, he had found, and now it was ripped away from him without mercy. He couldn't help replay the horrific scene, where his father was shot dead, and his brother left for dead. He worried for Dakota's safety, as he knew, through word spreading in jail as well as the media, that he too, was on the run.

9

LAKOTA DRIED IN THE SUN ALONG WITH HIS COMMANDEERED CLOTH-
ing and managed to slip into the city of San Francisco without being detected. He ripped the sleeves of the shirt off so as to alter his
appearance, but that didn't matter, he was paranoid out of his mind
and rightfully so. Everywhere he looked on the busy, sloped streets
he saw people's wandering eyes, certain they were eyeing him as he
tried to keep his head low and walk fast to an uncertain destination.
He rounded a corner and there were a couple of cop cars pulled up
to one another, and Lakota's heart started to pound as he was sure
they spotted him. So, he nonchalantly turned around and kept going
down the original street he was traveling. The police took notice
of his suspicious turnaround and Lakota was soon privy to their
potential curiosity, as he saw them driving opposite directions of
one another on a parallel street to Lakota. In a panic Lakota ran
across the street, further from the police, was nearly run over by a
trolley car, and then heard the loud ringing of church bells, telling
of the time. He sprinted towards the church, which was not far at
all, and sought out a hiding place within its gates and garden walls.
He hopped over a small fence and up ahead in the distance was a

large brown box with a tiled roof, so he sprinted for it. Its doors were unlocked, so he entered the shed. He quickly closed the door behind himself. It was pitch dark but once his eyes adjusted he could see around. It was a donation shed, stocked full of clothing, canned goods, candy, and various other items. He sat in silence for the next half hour until his paranoia momentarily subsided. He could tell it was getting darker as the temperature dropped and the little bit of light that made its way through the cracks dwindled to nearly nothing. He started to move about the shed when he heard footsteps. He quickly and quietly hid in and among the bags of donated clothes. The door swung open as Lakota looked from a crack. A sack of clothes was thrown right on top of him, and then the door was shut and locked. A relieved yet concerned Lakota freed himself from the sacks and prepared for his escape from the God-sent wooden box.

Two months had passed since Dakota crawled desperately hanging on to life into the thick of the woods at the base of the Rocky Mountains. He had managed to survive his gun shot and was steadily making his getaway to the north. It was the beginning of September and the weather was steadily dropping. He wore a rabbit fur and deer skin coat and carried a bow that he had made, along with a quiver of arrows. He wore deer skin pants and carried dried venison in his makeshift backpack as he headed north to Canada. It was his best option. He could get into Canada quicker, and it was less obvious of an escape. Dakota mourned the loss of his family as the cold air whipped across his face, but like the creeping cold his heart began to slip into a frigid state, much as it has been his entire life. So, he put his head down, dug his walking stick into the ground and walked on.

Panther's body was demanded by the Sioux Nation to be returned to the reservation, where he was buried and laid to rest next to his family. A great ceremony took place, ushering in the great ancestors to take Panther in the Sun to the land of his forefathers, a land of peace, a land where the buffalo ran free, a place where he could overlook his children hand-in-hand with Anna and a place where there was no longer pain. The dancing went on into the night, chanting, and the beating of drums like a heart that would never die. He had come for his children, and was still walking with them as they struggled. The fire burnt through the night, lighting the night sky with prayers and power for the once-again lost children.

Lakota waited until all noises from around the church subsided and began rummaging in the dark through the various sacks within the shed. In no time at all he had a clean pair of boxer shorts, pants, a shirt, a sweater, a scarf, some socks, a pair of boots, a jacket, a hat and a backpack that he loaded with all sorts of donated stuff including canned food, candles, etc. as well as extra clothing and a blanket. Now all he had to do was get out of the locked shed, which was relatively simple seeing that he had come this far. In no time at all he managed to unscrew the bolts that held the lock together from the inside using a bottle opener, which he gladly packed away in his sack. He quietly exited the shed, thankful for the donations, and made his way through the city an undetectable man. He had one thing on his mind, and one thing only: Sarah, and his unborn child. He knew exactly where she was, but didn't exactly know how to go about getting there. All he had was a pack of supplies, his feet beneath him, and empty pockets. But, above all of these this, he had determination fueled by love. And nothing, absolutely nothing, was going to stop him from getting to Sarah. He walked into the night and traveled straight east towards Chicago.

John and Charlie were in all of the newspapers around the country. In Chicago, John's adopted family, the Rosenthal family, were torn to pieces over the recent events. They now knew that both their son and his newly found brother, who was previously presumed dead, were now being hunted down. They had been in contact with Dakota's adopted family for quite some time, and they too were nearly destroyed about the thought of their son left for dead, but now missing and wanted. Sarah was back home with her mother and father in the outskirts of the city of Chicago. Their home was going to be under constant surveillance for any sight of John. Sarah was pregnant and under house arrest.

"I know one thing, for damned sure, if he tries to come around here, he'll have a twelve gauge waitin' for 'im!" Sarah's father said from his recliner, drunk as usual.

"He's a good man, daddy!" Sarah yelled back to him from her seat on the couch.

"Was being the key word. Up and takes my daughter to God knows where. Kills an innocent man . . . now a damn fugitive!" he said with slanted brows.

"An innocent man! An innocent man! How dare you! That man was going to rape me! I have no idea how mom puts up with you!" she yelled as her mother came out of the kitchen.

"What'd you say?" he abruptly rose from his chair. "Puts up with me?" he rushed Sarah who was standing close to the living room wall. Sarah tried to quickly move, but he got a hold of her before she could get away. He grabbed her by the throat and put her against the wall.

"Gary! Stop! Stop it!" Sarah's mom tried to pry his hands from her throat and pull his arms down to no avail. He took one hand away from Sarah, and shoved his wife to the floor.

"Don't you ever speak to me that way again!" he yelled as Sarah started to turn all shades of color. Sarah managed a nod, and he let her go. Sarah slid down the wall.

"That's it Gary! That's it! I'm calling in one of those officers right now!" Betty exclaimed with great intensity behind her blue eyes and with a pointed finger. She stood firm.

"O.k. then I'll just have to kill us all right now. Including that little mixed breed little mutt in our precious daughter's gut. I'm not scared a' hell, better than here. Go ahead."

"Mom, don't, please, don't," Sarah said as tears welled in her eyes as she sat helplessly on the floor. Sarah's mom looked at her, and could see the fear—a fear she knew all too well. A real fear.

"Yeah, that's what I thought," Gary said and then moved slowly with a stagger back to his recliner.

"O.k. daddy, you're right. I'm gonna go up to bed . . . it's late."

"Oh, honey . . . let me help you up," Betty said as she helped Sarah up and then up the stairs to her room. They got into Sarah's bedroom and they both sat on the edge of the bed. They spoke quietly.

"I'm gonna get you away from dad, just as soon as I can," Sarah said as she looked deep into her mom's eyes.

"There's no way, Sarah. There's never been. And now, no way. You're gonna have a baby and . . ."

"Exactly, that's why me and you are gonna get away from him forever. I know John's coming for me. There's no way I'm raising a baby here, and there's no way I'm leaving you here with dad. He's got you trapped in fear, mom."

"Well, if you haven't noticed, the police are crawling around everywhere. And how do you know John's coming? Even if he did make it, there'd be no way," Sarah's mom said shaking her head. "It's nonsense."

"It's nonsense to continue living like this. I swear on the life of our baby that John will make a way."

"You need to give up false hope, honey. You're under house arrest first of all. . . ."

"Yeah, well, so are you."

It seemed too good to be true as Lakota made his way without a single snag along the way. But snags are inevitable, and he was just waiting for the floor to drop out from underneath him, as it should have. But he had done it, so far, and no floors were dropping. He was walking steady like a marathon in which the finish line was the only life line he had remaining in his life. He thought often as he traveled of the great race, two brothers, unknown to one another, and he felt warm at the thought of Dakota running at full speed. Lakota's race, like the childhood race, was once again measured and timed. He knew that if he just kept running that he'd win, no matter what. He wasn't running or walking in fear or sadness, but in peace at the union forged, though cut short, with his brother and father, and now to his own son. A journey his father once made for him, he was doing for his own.

A focus and intellect that came with his determination guided every step of the way to Chicago. He walked through whipping October wind knowing that he would soon be with Sarah and their child. He knew the facts. He knew about the manhunt. He knew about the indefinite barricade that would be patrolling his destination, but with every step he thought out each and every future step that he would make to rescue Sarah, and make their escape once again.

State lines came and went as Lakota trekked eastward mainly on foot, travelling through countryside and occasionally hopping trains. As he steamed forward he thought of his brother, now that he knew he was alive from seeing newspaper headlines, and on the run as well. He longed to see him.

Just as Lakota was thinking of him, Dakota was doing the same.

Dakota felt lost in every sense of the term. All that he knew was that he was alone, sad, cold, and confused. But, like his brother, he was still focused. This was a trait they seemed to create out of necessity and a state of mind they both knew. It's just that they both finally found better—better than the original cards they had been dealt, and that's all Dakota wanted back. And that, too, was his driving force as he bided his time in Canada. He dreamt of the warmth of the Mexican village. When the time was right, this was going to be his move. Until then, he was alone, but alive. He had no clue as to the fate of John and Sarah, seeing that he avoided any and all small towns he remotely came in proximity to. He naturally imagined the worst. John in prison, Sarah too. He had no idea. He would not, however, concede to the worst, and in his mind as well as heart walked in the warm sunshine of their company and love as he traveled along.

Sarah bided her time. Her doctor said the baby would be due mid-April, and it was now the first of November. Sarah was already deeply in love with her and John's baby, and was now just waiting for John. She could care less where the baby was born, as long as John was there. The police steadily dwindled from the neighborhood, and Sarah just knew John was near.

"Mom, you're coming with us," Sarah said to her mom as they sat on Sarah's bed.

"Sarah, he is not coming. You are not having this baby on the run!" she yelled in a whisper, so as to not attract attention.

"Mom, I would rather have the baby on the run than let the beast downstairs even take one single look at my baby. He's already hit you twice this month; imagine when there's a screaming little bundle of joy interrupting his damn radio programs. He'll hit us both, and probably the baby too. If John's not here in a week, then me and you are taking the emergency money right out from under dad's nose and running. I know what I'm doing."

"Oh is that right? You are losing it, Sarah. There's no way I'm letting this happen. What do you know about child birth?"

"For your information mom . . . I've assisted a woman in birth. I am a different woman now, mom. I am more Sioux than white."

"Sioux, huh?"

"In my heart. You know what? I don't care what you do. Stay locked in chains. Continue to be emotionally and physically abused . . . be my guest. But I'll be damned if I stick around. . . ." Just then Gary walked in drunk as ever.

"Stick around what? What you all talkin' about? Huh? Talkin' about me? Huh?" he said as he grabbed Betty by the back of her hair. "Huh woman?"

"Nothing daddy."

"Nothing daddy . . . nothing daddy . . . you're a damn liar, Sarah! You ain't goin' nowhere, if that's what you're thinking. Nowhere. Got it?" he let go of Betty's hair and got into Sarah's face.

"Yeah, got it dad. Got it," she said to avoid any violence.

"Good. Now, c'mon, Betty. It's time for bed." Gary walked out of the room and Betty gave Sarah a look that spoke a thousand words. Eyes that were ready to leave.

John had been in Chicago, in the actual neighborhood for the last two days, spying on the house, plotting their escape. He had already set up their escape route, and made means for transportation. His only thought, was south. North was an unforgiving winter, and if his baby was going to have a chance, then south was the only direction. Plus, it would be the least expected direction and border to watch. The cops had dispersed, and he got the courage to make his move. It was midnight and John started throwing little pebbles to what he knew was Sarah's window. The lights were out as Sarah slept in a deep dream. Not one pebble was heard, as John threw from the bushes. So, he found a tree. And he climbed that tree. And he attracted attention. A night owl neighbor on the specific look out for just this type of situation. It was no secret. John was a wanted man. And this gentleman didn't want to call no cops, nah, this was his moment to shine. So the man moved for his shotgun, as John had finally made it to the window. John knocked, and knocked. The man slowly, as if savoring the moment, moved to his closet, and loaded his shotgun. Stirring, then awake, Sarah popped up out of bed, knew it was John, grabbed her bag, full of the emergency money she had already taken as soon as her father passed out that very evening, ripped open the window and let John in. Blast! The man took a shot at John and missed just by inches, as his feet barely fell into the window.

"John!" Sarah started to cry and grabbed onto John.

"No time, let's go! Down the stairs, out the front!" Lights in the neighborhood came on, dogs started barking.

"My dad's down there, no way. And my mom, my mom . . . she's coming too!"

"Alright, get your mom, now! Where's your dad?" he said in a loud whisper with wide eyes.

"He's asleep downstairs on the chair," Sarah said in a panic.

"Get your mom, meet me downstairs. Hurry!" John ran downstairs with warrior eyes, ready to kill, ready to do whatever the situation called for. The neighbor ran down his own stairs at the same time, gun in hand. John flew down the stairs and was met by a drunk Gary with a shotgun. John didn't stop. He slid like a torpedo, feet first into Gary, taking him out with a lightning strike to the knees as he stood on the living room floor. John popped up, took the gun from the stunned, knocked down drunk, and then delivered a blow to his head.

"John! John! We're ready!" Sarah yelled as she and her mom came running down the stairs.

"Keys, car keys!" John yelled as the neighbor shot a hole in the backdoor.

"I've got them, let's go, garage!" Sarah yelled as she frantically opened the door to the garage. John ripped off the license plate as if it were aluminum foil, flung the garage door open like it was made of cardboard, and then jumped into the vehicle and they tore out of the garage like a bat out of a cave. The old man, in one last desperado wanna-be-hero attempt, shot wildly at the speeding car to no avail. It was then that he ran back into his house and called the cops.

"This is not good. Oh my God, this is not good. This is bad, this is . . . oh my God, Sarah, what the hell are we doing . . . we're gonna get caught, killed . . . oh my . . ." Betty was panicking, needless to say. She couldn't stop shaking and started to cry hysterically. John just looked at Sarah.

"It's o.k. mom. We're gonna make it. You will never be hit again. You will never be treated like that again, mom! O.k.! Listen to me . . . mom," Sarah got less stern and loud. "John's here. We're free."

"Is she right, John?"

"Yes ma'am. Nothing can stop us now. The path has been laid before us. A path of freedom. Now, hold on tight, cause I'm gonna have to gallop."

"Where to, baby?" Sarah asked with scared eyes.

"I've got it all mapped out. We just got to get you outta here. How's our baby?"

"Kickin', wanting to run," Sarah said as she put her hand on her belly, and her other hand on John's. She gave him a little smile, with melting eyes.

"John, John, I really hope you know what you're doing . . . I mean, . . ." Betty spoke frantically as she looked all around. "You know they're coming for us. They know this car, John."

"I know. It's o.k., we're only in the car for another few minutes."

"Huh?" Sarah said with confused, scared eyes for John.

"Let's just say you'll be riding with me Sarah, unless of course you can't ride a horse, mom."

"Mom?" Betty asked.

"Yeah, mom, can you ride?" John said as he looked in the rear view mirror.

"I mean, well, no."

"O.k. you'll ride with me. Sarah, can you manage?"

"Yeah, but where did you get horses, and why horses?"

"I borrowed them, and it's how we're getting out of here. I got two tied up in a patch of woods. We're going south. Winter is in the north, and they'll be expecting us to go north."

"That's either the stupidest thing or smartest thing. I have no idea at this point, John," Sarah said as she looked all around and that's when distant police sirens could be heard.

"Trust me. There's no way we could survive the winter on the run. Thank God, you guys live on the edge of the city. I staked it all out. There's a rock quarry right near where the spot is, that's where we can ditch the car. We'll walk the stream, so as to not leave tracks, then hop on the horses," John said driving at breakneck speed, taking sharp curves and turns like he was some sort of professional getaway driver.

"O.k., o.k., are we almost there, or what?" Sarah asked as she looked back at her mom.

"Yeah, there's a dirt road coming up in just a half mile. We got this. Trust me."

"O.k."

John pulled off onto an abandoned dirt road with the cops only minutes behind them. He instructed the girls to get out when they reached the large quarry, then he jammed the gas pedal with an ice scraper and let the car drive itself over the edge. It met about ten feet of water when it landed and by then they were all running full speed, all hand-in-hand to the horses. Sarah had ridden before, in Mexico, so she was ready and willing to hop up and go. John helped Betty onto the horse, told her to hold on, and then led them all away in a fast canter. With the city far behind them, they made their escape. Within no time at all, they were at the shallow creek, deep within evergreens and maples that John had spoken of and walked their horses for miles heading south downstream to an already well-thought-out route by John. Their destination— Mexico.

A massive search team was in hot pursuit of the crew. Dogs, cops, volunteers, search planes, etc. etc. were all beating down their path, but lost them at the stream a good twenty minutes behind the fleeing family. John's plan was to run then walk, run then walk the horses and then when the horses could go no more, they would take to foot. South of Chicago was all farm land, and forest. And south was the only way he was willing to take Sarah. He would do anything to get them across the border, and he carried a pistol with plenty of ammo to make sure that happened. He wasn't sure what was ahead of them, but all he knew was that the path was going to be lit up for them to show the way.

There was no time for sleep, and when the horses had no more to give they took to foot as planned. They tried to walk as fast as possible and with mindfulness as to where they stepped so as to not leave many prints, which was a very hard thing to do. A rock, a patch of leaves . . . they basically tried not to leave any real footprints. But the dogs weren't tracking footprints, and they could hear them far off in many directions barking at the excitement of the hunt. Before long they came across a farm house with a large barn as they poked their heads out of the woods. John pulled out his pistol and told the girls to stay put. He stealthfully ran to the barn, just to get a better look at the house. He peered into the barn, and there it was, an airplane. John's jaw dropped, and his heart started to beat. Maybe he would be sympathetic? The case is nationwide, whoever owns this plane might be sympathetic John thought, as he motioned to the girls to run his way.

"Alright, stay here, next to this barn. Our ticket out of here might be in this barn. I'm going for the man who owns it," John said with intensity in his eyes.

"What?" Sarah asked as she looked at John scared and puzzled and then looked into the small barn window. "Oh my God." And with that John moved towards the small home. His heart pounded, his breath became short and he was on the verge of a panic attack as he squatted down in a bush next to a window and checked his weapon. He took a breath and slowly lifted up to look with a hidden eye into the home. He saw an older man, about sixty, and what looked to be his wife. He knew what he had to do, and now was the time. He looked out to the front of the home and saw a long, home-beat, homemade, once-was, landing strip. He motioned for Sarah and Betty to come running, and then they all stood in front of the door. John rang the bell. And within a half-minute, after pulling back the shade to have a look at the visitors, the old man opened the door. John immediately held the gun up to the man.

"Sir, I'm a desperate man."

"Apparently so," he said without fear. "I know who you are. Please, come in."

"Huh?"

"Yeah, I've been following the story. Please come in. Honey, make some tea."

John was shocked, as they all were. They stood at this man's door dirty, exhausted, scared, wanted, and he just invited them in.

"O.k., yes sir." John was still apprehensive, and so he kept the gun pointed. "The gun . . . I can't take any chances, sir."

"I understand. I also understand you are a naval officer and an innocent man," the kind man said as he guided them to the sofa. "Looks like you're gonna be a momma sweetheart," he said as he gave Sarah a little smile.

"Yes, sir," she said with a little smile back followed by a tear that she quickly wiped away.

"Oh, no, it's o.k. I'm Harold and that's my wife Katherine."

"Hello," she spoke loudly from the kitchen. "Are you all hungry?"

"I mean, well . . ."

"Yes, honey, they sure are."

"Why would you let us in?" Betty asked puzzled as she felt like she was in some kind of strange dream.

"We like good people. So, now, how can we help?" the man said as he sat back in his rocker and lit his pipe.

"Are you serious, sir, I mean Harold, because we need help . . . I mean we really need help."

"O.k., well. Where do you need to go?"

"As close to the Mexican border as possible, if not over. And time is not on our side."

"Well, did you see the plane?"

"Yes, sir."

"Can you fly?"

John choked on his tea. "Mmmuh," he vocalized as he cleared his throat. "No, but I know some basics from fly boys on my ship."

"Alright, you're gonna take that plane. It's yours. I'll show you how to fly it."

"What?! Now hang on. Maybe you have a car we could borrow?"

"Nope. We don't drive anymore. Eyesight, you know. The plane, well, let's just say I don't fly anymore. I built it myself, but then got arthritis," he said as he moved his arm at his elbow with a little wince.

"Oh my God, we're gonna die," Betty said as she looked around the room, not believing what she was hearing.

"Yeah, it's true . . . he built that thing. It's a good plane. He's so inventive," Katherine said. "It's simple to fly. I've taken the stick many times."

"O.k., let's go," John said. "Please."

They all went out to the barn, Harold unlocked the sliding doors, and they all stepped in.

"Seats—two in back, then pilot and co-pilot seats. Propellers here, guns below," Harold explained as a matter of fact. "It'll outrun anything in the sky. And those planes are far from here anyway, you lost them in the air tonight, nice work. Alright John, let's hop in. I've got plenty of fuel. Shoot, I've got enough fuel for you to fly to Europe. All of the spare fuel is in the cargo bay. But the tank can only hold so much. I'm not exactly sure how far you will get before needing to refuel. There are many factors that will determine that. But I built it with a huge fuel tank. So."

"Hang on," John said as Harold pulled down the stairs to the medium sized plane. "I'm not so sure." John looked at Sarah, her belly, and then at Betty.

"Yeah, he's not so sure," Betty said.

"Oh, alright. Yeah, no problem, let's just forget about it," Harold said nonchalantly.

"No. No, I got it. Show me, Harold, but the quick and simple version please," John said. "We can get all the way to Mexico?"

"Maybe."

"Alright, alright," John said with a little bit of a crazy laugh.

"Dear God," Betty said as she climbed in after everyone, sat next to Sarah, and then looked back at Katherine standing in the barn, who was just smiling. Within fifteen minutes Harold broke down the essentials to John who was concentrating like never before. He truly had heard most of what Harold was saying, and actually took the stick with a navy pilot on a little night test flight.

"One last thing, John," Harold said with now a more serious tone. "People don't just go flying whenever and wherever they want. There is protocol for all flights. Permission, etc. But, since you're on the run, you can't call in a flight plan. So, we are going to turn off your radio. A nice silent flight. And, here, it's the manual for the plane. Just in case. Good luck, John." Harold gave him a smile and extended his hand for John to shake. John shook his hand and thanked him. Katherine threw in a duffle bag of supplies and at minute twenty the props were started and they were on the run way. Betty was in hysterics and John was at the stick. John turned and nodded a thank you to the smiling couple.

"Alright girls, hang on!" John exclaimed as he pushed the throttle full force forward and at a hundred miles an hour he pulled back on his controls after bumping and shaking for the last two hundred yards and they lifted off. "I'm not gonna fail you girls! I swear to God! And we've got guns on this thing!" Betty started hooting and hollering, then started to laugh within a cry.

"This is crazy!" She yelled and then they all started laughing in an exhausted yet adrenaline pumped way, verging on insanely manner.

"Yeah! Ha, ha, ha!" John exclaimed as he looked out of the front cockpit window. "Yeah," he said as he quickly got serious and the focus returned. They elevated to eight thousand feet as the sun came up. John flew southwest, without an aircraft in the sky. They were all bundled up in warm gear and breathing in fresh oxygen, all designed and stocked by the kind man who built a plane. The cockpit was equalized, and semi-heated, an impressive feat for planes of the time, and everything was flying smoothly.

The search party showed up at Harold and Katherine's door at dawn asking every sort of question, and they got their answers. Harold recounted every last detail, with manufactured residual fear in his voice, as did Katherine, as to how they barged in and put them to the floor with the gun. Harold then told them that they cut their phone line (which Harold did himself after they left) and recounted how they locked them in the basement, but how they escaped out of the basement by picking the lock only moments before the authorities arrived. He then told them that he could hear the fugitives arguing outside the basement door about whether or not to take the plane. He then went on to tell them that they finally decided to, that the man knew enough about flying, and that they were headed to Canada. So, without wasting any time, the search party headed north with all of their planes they had at their disposal, trusting in every word the honest man told them. After all, the Canadian border was much closer than the Mexican border.

As Lakota, Sarah, and Betty flew towards freedom, Dakota stepped out onto the snow-covered ground from an old abandoned cabin that sat deep in the woods next to a small, nearly frozen, stream. It was his new home. He had spent the last month cleaning it out and fixing it up, and had decided that he should ride the winter out here, spending at least a few more months in hiding before he decided to move on. And, in all reality, he had no idea what or where that would look like. He had nothing or no one to inspire a move or a direction to travel. The sadness hung over Dakota's head, and weighted his heart like he had never experienced before. And he couldn't pinpoint one specific emotion, it was as if they were all locked once again. He was just surviving. Just living, and wasn't sure why. He fell asleep at night the same as the nights before . . . hopeless. His dreams were dead. And it all started with a letter. If only he would have been oblivious to his father and brother. He wished he had never met them, nor loved them, nor been loved by them. Then maybe he could have gone back to a normal life, a life he knew before the war, before he knew he had a real family. The saying that "it is better to have loved and lost than never loved at all" only pissed him off, as it repeated like an obsessive thought in his mind. He wished he had never loved at all.

"How long to Mexico, John?" Betty spoke above the loud propellers.

"Oh, I don't know, about four hours. We're going two hundred and fifty miles an hour, so I'd say we're making good time!" John answered back loudly. "How are you feeling, Sarah?!"

"Great!" she said and then gave John a little sarcastic smile, as John looked back.

"O.k., well just hang in there. We'll be there soon."

"Where are we planning on landing, John?" Betty asked as she climbed into the co-pilot's chair. "I mean it's not like we're just gonna fly into the Mexico City airport."

"We're gonna have to figure that out once we get there. I'm gonna bring us in on the east coast, and we'll just look for a field to land in."

"Yeah, like a coca field or marijuana field," Betty said sarcastically.

"Yep, that's why we have the guns," John said with a smile for Betty who just gave John a look.

"Well at least Gary's not here." Betty said as she looked at John and Sarah to see their reaction.

"Yeah, he abused us both . . . he's an awful man, and you did the right thing!" Sarah said as she scooted herself up between her and John.

"O.k., looks like some weather ahead girls," John said plainly.

"Huh?" Betty said as she turned and looked out the front window and saw a giant black mass hovering in the sky.

"Oh my God, John," Sarah said as she put her hand on his arm.

"It's o.k., maybe we can fly around it, or under. Maybe even over it," John said optimistically an hour into an only smooth flight.

"O.k., yeah, o.k." Sarah said with a look of fear, and Betty just nodded in agreement.

"Yeah, o.k."

"Why don't you get back there with Sarah, and strap in. O.k. Betty?"

"Yeah, sure John," she said as she maneuvered back into her seat.

"Well, I don't know, it's moving at us fast, and we're moving at it faster. It looks like the only way is straight through. Up is black, and down is . . . ." he was cut off by major turbulence followed by a flash of lighting that was followed by a sonic boom that came only one second after the bright strike.

"Oh my God, John!" Sarah was terrified, and Betty started to whimper as she held onto Sarah's arm.

"It's o.k.! It's o.k.! We're gonna make it through! Hopefully it's just a small storm!" John's heart was racing as he gripped the controls with all of his strength, as the wind tried to rip them from his sweating hands. The black was starting to envelope them, and soon it was pitch black in what was once a sunny morning. John was flying blind and had only his instruments to rely on. He kept a constant altitude, made sure his bearing was on track, and monitored his radar for any oncoming aircraft. The turbulence only got worse, tossing the plane about like a balsa wood toy in a light wind.

"John," Sarah said with a quivering and literally shaking voice.

"I know, we'll make it, just sit tight!" John fought with the stick desperately trying to keep the plane level. The storm raged for a half hour and just as soon as it started, it stopped. The sun blasted its rays into the cockpit and passenger windows.

"Thank God!" Betty exclaimed.

"Yeah, oh my God," Sarah said in discomfort yet relief.

"O.k. girls, we're in the silver lining."

"Yep, onto the coca fields!" Betty said with a fist aiming forward. They all went silent, and then burst out into hysterical laughter that went on for a good five minutes with tears of joy and exhaustion.

10

CHARLIE WOKE UP AND DID WHAT HE ALWAYS DID IN THE MORNING, except a new peace was coming over him. He rose from his wooden framed bed furnished with a worn-out dirty mattress that he covered up with animal furs and walked out into a sunny, cold, Canadian winter to piss in the snow, and while he was peeing he smiled. He felt a warmth and was glad that he had been loved. He even laughed a little at the thought of everyone. Just as he was shaking free the last drops, he heard footsteps coming up behind him. He quickly turned around, and there stood the most beautiful thing Charlie had ever seen. A young woman. As if sent from heaven as the sun lit her face and sparkled off the crisp stream behind her.

"Uh, hi," Charlie said slightly embarrassed as he tucked his member back into his pants, while covering his eyes from the rising sun. The girl said nothing, but just looked. Charlie walked closer to her, and she stepped further back. "It's o.k., I'm not going to hurt you. I'm a good man," he said to the clearly not understanding Native American woman dressed in animal furs and moccasin boots. Her hair was braided back into two sections and her eyes were an inviting, innocent brown. Charlie slowly moved closer to her. She put her hand onto her side, where she wore a hand crafted hunting knife. "Whoa, whoa! O.k. I'll back up." Charlie slowly moved back and then found a rock to sit on. That's when the young woman moved closer to Charlie. She got close enough to him, so as to check him out. He looked a lot like her. "It's o.k.," Charlie smiled and she smiled back. She found a rock to sit on directly across from him. Charlie hadn't seen anyone in a long time, and he was thrilled to have company, even if she didn't understand him. "This is my home," Charlie said as he pointed to the cabin. She nodded yes and smiled. "Where is your home?" Charlie said while pointing to the cabin, then her and then shrugging while he pointed in all directions. "Where are you from?" Charlie didn't expect an answer, but then she made a picture in the snow. He watched as she drew with her finger. He slowly moved closer. She stopped and quickly moved back. "It's o.k." Charlie said verbally and with his eyes as he showed his hands. "I want to look," he said as he looked down on the ground. She moved back and finished the picture.

When Charlie looked at the picture, it nearly brought him to tears. In it was a little girl with a circle drawn around her and a giant x drawn over the girl's family, her mother, her father, and her two brothers. Alongside that picture the young woman drew three men with rifles. She then looked up from the picture with a tear in her eye, and pointed to the little girl then to herself. Then she wiped the picture away and drew another picture depicting her running through the forest with the men chasing after her. Then, she wiped the picture away. The next picture was of her hiding in a cave, all alone, with a frown and tear upon her face. She looked up again at Charlie who was now unable to stop the welling tears, and a tear fell onto her picture in the snow. He then drew his own series of pictures and at their conclusion the young woman looked up at Charlie. Their eyes met, locked, and understood. Charlie reached out his hand to the young woman and she delicately placed her hand in his. They got up from their rocks, and Charlie guided her into his home.

John and his crew were making good progress as the plane soared smoothly along. "It's lookin' good, ladies," John said confidently, especially now that he could see.

"How do you know where to go?" Betty asked as she got back in the cockpit.

"I'm trained in these types of things ma'am."

"From the air?"

"Well, it's about the same. I know our roundabout coordinates, and we should actually be there in only a few hours."

"And where is there?"

"Cabo Rojo."

"Oh, nice. Why there, and what does that mean?"

"I don't know. I just know that it's on the eastern coast of Mexico . . . I think rojo is red in Spanish."

"Oh great, it's probably referring to blood. Nice choice, John," she said sarcastically and backhanded his upper arm.

"No, no! I think that's sangre, mom!" Sarah said from the back rather loudly. "Anyone want a sandwich?"

"Yeah! Thanks, baby!" John waited for a sandwich to be passed forward.

"Well, all this talk of blood is making me hungry; so sure," Betty said with a smile for her daughter.

"Isn't this exciting, mom!"

"Exciting is not the word for it, honey."

John's plan was to overshoot the little stretch of land that was Cabo Rojo, which was the Red Cape, and really only a beach. His plan was to land the plane in the desert that laid behind. And if everything went smoothly, they would quickly make it out on foot with all of the supplies Harold so kindly bestowed upon them and make it into a small village, then onto their good friends on the west coast. They were only an hour out, when the unexpected, or maybe expected, happened. The fuel light came on and even though they had fuel on board, they had no way of refueling mid-flight. John kept this to himself, so as not to alarm the girls. He hoped that the plane's reserve tank was of significant size to make it. They had been flying over the gulf for the last forty-five minutes and it was nothing but open water. He thought about taking a more northern course, but knew that his best chance to land without notice and with flat ground was in the flatlands behind Cabo Rojo. So he stayed on course. The girls were both in the back, fast asleep, exhausted from the entire experience, and John was beginning to worry. He silenced the beeping fuel light, but watched as the gauge steadily dropped below empty. Another half hour passed, and the coast was now in sight. If he could just make it close enough, then they could maybe coast in. But, inevitably, the fuel ran out and both engines died, one after the other. It was then that loud alarms coupled by a flashing red light woke the girls. The plane fought against John and John fought back to keep it level. They rapidly lost elevation at nearly a forty-five-degree angle.

"John! What is it?" Sarah popped up at the same time as her mom.

"We're out of fuel . . . both engines are dead. Prepare for emergency landing. Find the life vests and life boat, as well as the survival pack," John said calmly but sternly with all of the seriousness necessary in the tone of his voice.

"What!" Betty started to panic and began to lose it. "Sarah, oh my God! We're going to die! We'll never make it!" She began to cry, and a crazy look came over her face and into her eyes as the plane fell from the sky.

"Mom! Listen! Help me find the life vests and boat, o.k.?"

"What, I mean, where, oh my God, what are we doing, we should have never . . ."

Sarah cut her short with a sudden and tight grip onto her mom's shoulders.

"Mom. Help me," Sarah said calmly while looking deep into her eyes with intensity.

"O.k., o.k. I can do this, I mean . . ."

"Yes, you can, now come on." They quickly found the life preservers and life boat as well as the survival pack.

"There are parachutes John!" Sarah yelled to John.

"We're too low! We'd hit the water before the chutes would pop! We're making a water landing! There's no other option! I've got this! I still have control over the plane, just no power!" John spoke with great adrenaline that was giving him great focus and confidence. "I'm just going to get us level, our speed will be down, and we'll come in like a duck." The plane was extremely quiet at this point, as the alarm finally quit. "Strap in. Get those vests on. I'll get mine on and when we hit the water we need to act quickly. O.k.?" The girls just sat silently and nodded. John looked back and saw the fear in their eyes. "We're going to make it. We've come this far; we're going to make it." The girls just nodded again and held on tight to one another's hands.

John fought the stick to keep the plane level against the torrent of wind currents. His heart was pounding, as the ocean drew nearer and nearer. And then, complete loss of control of the plane came as they neared a thousand feet. The plane started to tilt back and forth.

"Hold on!" John yelled. "I love you all!"

"Oh my God!" Betty screamed as they stopped spinning and dropped nose first like a rock towards the sea.

"I love you too, John!" Sarah yelled over the scream of the plane.

"Oh baby! My grandbaby! This isn't happening!" Betty grabbed on tight to Sarah. That's when the softest light came and a warmth came over the plane. John, Sarah, and Betty were suspended in a trance-like state where time did not exist, nor fear, nor sense of their physical bodies. A swift current of wind rushed under the plane coupled by a temporary soft glow within the plane, leveling it out and the plane touched down flat onto the water. The suspended state of being maintained, until a complete reality check hit all of them as the plane slammed into the water. The plane dipped to one side, ripping off the right wing and the plane drastically, abruptly lost speed throwing all of their bodies forward.

"Ah!" Sarah screamed as the safety belt ripped into her abdomen. The plane stopped as if it hit a wall, and everyone sprung to action. The plane started to tip to the left, and so the escape route was to the right. John quickly moved back to the hatch, popped it open, threw the boat into the sea, and had the girls quickly jump out before the plane went down. Within thirty seconds they were all in the water. John pulled the chord to the life raft and helped the girls in. They all looked back at the plane in shock but then snapped back to reality.

"Are you o.k. and our baby?" John asked while gasping for breath.

"Fine, fine," Sarah said with great amazement that they were alive. "Betty?"

Betty looked back at the now sinking plane and became overwhelmed with emotion. The gravity of the situation, as well as years and years of abuse, came to a head right then and there. She started balling uncontrollably as she sat in the bobbing life raft.

"Oh momma," Sarah's eyes spoke a thousand words as she moved to her mother's side and held onto her. She knew her pain. And words could not fix nor console. So she just held her and let her cry. She looked at John with a look of sadness for her mother. Lakota looked back with understanding and took a deep breath and let it go slowly as he took in the entirety of everything. He looked down, then out onto the sea. He nodded his head yes, answering his own self, and started to paddle to the distant shore.

Meanwhile, Charlie cooked breakfast for his new-found friend as the sun made its way into the one-window cabin. He placed a plate of canned berries and smoked venison with a glass of fresh mountain water in front of his new-found friend.

"Eat, it's good," Charlie motioned to the beautiful young woman sitting at his table. He couldn't help but smile. She happily ate and Charlie happily joined her. They both just smiled and chewed. "Berries," Charlie said with a smile. Then she spoke.

"Baaree," she said and took a bite.

"Yeah, Berry!" Charlie was so excited. Something so small meant the world to him. They shared a smile.

A three-quarters moon lit the ocean as they neared a tiny island covered with palm trees. The water calmed with the fall of night and within an hour they were on shore of some unknown island off the coast of Cabo Rojo. John hopped out of the boat and pulled the life raft ashore. He helped Betty and Sarah out onto solid ground.

"Now what, baby?" Sarah asked plainly and with a confidence in her voice.

"We rest. Let's set up camp for the night. The beach has nice coverage, so we can just find some palms and make a quick little shelter. I'll pull the raft into the bush, so no one can see it and we'll just get some sleep. We can head for the mainland at dawn. Sound good?" Lakota said as he started to get busy.

"Sounds good, John," Betty nodded, then made her way with Sarah to the tree line.

"Thank you, baby," Sarah gave John a tired smile and then a little kiss as she walked with her mom.

Morning came without incident. They awoke to a beautiful rising sun, cascading its light across the emerald water. They set a course for the mainland, and everyone paddled in silence across the glassy water. Within a few hours they landed on a beach that lead to a great span of desert. Lakota made a backpack from material off the lifeboat, and he filled it with all of the survival gear the boat provided. They walked with determination through the cactus-filled desert, only stopping for water and shade. The call of the forest in the distance kept them moving with purpose.

"I want you to know, John, and I really mean this," Betty said as she walked alongside John. "I know you're a good man," she said as she got ahead of John and faced him with her pretty blue eyes. They all stopped briefly. "What you have experienced in your short amount of time on earth is more than anyone should ever have to go through. We haven't spent much time together, but I want you to know that I see you. I just wanted you to know that, for what it's worth," she said with tears forming in her eyes. "And, thank you."

"I see you too Betty. I see you too," Lakota said with open arms. Betty wrapped her arms around him, and he did the same. "Thank you for raising such an amazing daughter." They both pulled back and shared a smile that they turned to Sarah who was already smiling.

"Let's go home," Lakota said with happiness in his voice, and they walked on. Lakota, Sarah, and Betty arrived to their once temporary home near the waterfall, and were welcomed with open arms.

Epilogue

DAKOTA BUILT A LOG HOME WITH HIS OWN TWO HANDS, LARGE enough for his new family deep in the Canadian Rockies. He had a two-year old boy and a six-month old little girl whom both gave him joy like never before. His mate for life, his love, stood by his side, as they forged a magnificent life. Dakota was at peace, fulfilled, and connected to his ancestors like never before, as he listened to the sounds of mother earth and savored every second of his blessed life. He was positive that John and Sarah had made their way, especially after hearing from a local trapper, a couple years back, that the man-hunt was called off for those "AWOL fugitives." He knew that they would meet again when the time was right, and he knew right where to find him. His father had come for him, had loved him, and would always live in Dakota's heart.

Lakota and Sarah became proud parents of two happy and healthy little boys. Wesley was four and Christopher was one. They both shared in the resemblance of their parents and were full of life and love. For the first time in many long years, Betty was living a life of freedom and joy. She had great purpose and even fell in love. Her heart was full and she cherished every day, not once looking back. Sarah was madly in love with her life. Her love for John and their children was everything. She would follow John to the moon, but was so happy to have a home.

Lakota was full of peace. Being a father, a husband, a brother, a son, and an important member of his tribe gave him great joy. He would often sit on a rock where his brother and father once played at the pool of the waterfall. He could hear their voices and laughter harmonized with the pounding, ever-flowing water. His own children and the children of the tribe would now play in these same waters. He was often visited by a jet black panther with striking green eyes. The elusive creature would purposefully make itself known, only to Lakota, in a patch of sun. They would lock eyes with a knowingness and then the panther would slowly turn and walk away into the jungle, and Lakota would smile.

CPSIA information can be obtained
at www.ICGtesting.com
Printed in the USA
FSOW02n1302141216
28587FS